The
Sea
Of
Ash

by

Scott Thomas

Read *The Lovecraft eZine*, a free
online magazine featuring
Weird Fiction, Cosmic Horror,
and the Cthulhu Mythos:
www.LovecraftZine.com

Table of Contents

Editor's Preface

Never had the universe felt so vast, and I so small within it. I had, through circumstance, been made aware of something, but of what? Something either too horrible or too beautiful for humans to know.
—From *The Sea of Ash*

In my capacity as editor of *The Lovecraft eZine*, many books are sent to me in the hope that I will enjoy and promote them. And many of them are wonderful, to be sure. But in the four years that I've been publishing the *eZine*, no book has impressed me as much as *The Sea of Ash*, by Scott Thomas.

Scott gave me a copy of this novella in August 2013 at NecronomiCon (a Lovecraft convention held every two years in Providence), and I read it on the plane ride back home.

I don't remember much about that flight. *The Sea of Ash* utterly and completely captured my imagination. At once disturbing and beautiful, it is a fresh take on the themes of Lovecraft and cosmic horror. I am not exaggerating when I say that it is one of the best books I have ever read.

For the complete story on how *The Sea of Ash* came to be, read Jeff Thomas' Afterword. For now, suffice it to say that I soon realized that *The Sea of Ash* wasn't widely read, and it certainly deserves to be. After reading it, I think you will agree.

There is a world beneath the world, and the universe is not what it seems. Turn the page, and begin a journey into wonder.

Mike Davis
Editor/Publisher, *The Lovecraft eZine*
September, 2014

1. QUEEN ANNE

The photograph is a sepia thing showing Dr. Albert Pond shortly before his disappearance in 1920. He's handsome enough, clean shaven, with even features and slick dark hair parted above his high forehead. A serious fellow to be sure, looking a touch older than his forty-four years. I hold the picture closer and study his eyes. Intelligent eyes, keen eyes, their sting tempered by weariness, as if they have seen more than human eyes are meant to see.

By contrast, the photo I took of his family home is colored and bright, snapped in the warm flush of afternoon. I HAD to start there, after all, for a sense of completeness. Originally the Whitman parsonage, the house was built in Eastborough, Massachusetts in the mid-eighteenth century. It's a fine center hall Colonial with sparrow-beckoning chimneys, and ancient clapboards infused with generations of paint from Whitmans, and the Ponds that followed.

This is a ritual stillness, this sitting at my desk with the pictures, my gear ready and packed for the journey. I am stirring myself, inspiring myself, tuning in. I've waited years for this.

Now I am gazing at the only surviving photograph of the baby. The thick paper is brittle and brown with age, more so for the fire that ate away the left side -- the part that showed the child's head. How unfortunate. The babe is a shadowy blur, unclothed, the rounded limbs like sausage links. It lies limp in a rumpled puddle of blankets, as described in Dr. Pond's writings.

I have never seen a picture of the child's mother, though it is said that she, unlike her offspring, was uncommonly beautiful.

"I find it difficult to imagine a childhood more mundane," Albert reflected in the early pages of his single published work. And... "Perhaps that was the appeal."

The same can be said of mine. It was comfortingly unspectacular; you might even say insular. I was raised by my grandmother, just four and three-quarter miles from the house where the good Doctor grew up. That explains some of the kindredness I feel.

Nana was a naturalist. She would likely have been a Luddite if she had been born in London. While the front lawn of our house was an insignificant little square, the back was a glorious jumble of vegetation, deep and green, flowered and ferned. It was like a library of plants, and she knew all their names, both the charming folksy ones and the exotic Latin designations that sounded to me like snippets of magical incantations.

Whereas my siblings were imaginary, Pond had three sisters, one older, two younger. Samantha, Hope and Annie. His predilection for the healing arts manifested quite early -- he became a master doll mender to the girls. A curious aside...Annie's favorite doll (the one with long red human hair) would be found facing east whenever it rained.

Following his quiet childhood, Albert Pond went on to study at the best colleges, earning his medical degree with honors. He drifted up the coast, settled in Salisbury on the North Shore, and opened his practice.

In the snow of 1906 he met Bethany Miller. She was watching the Atlantic, watching the boats turn white, listening as gulls called to the snow, became snow. That silver afternoon, before dusk reared up from the sea, they walked and laughed under flakes and wings. Pond later noted that his heart was "fumbling and exhilarated." It also "felt lighter in my chest, a younger man's heart borrowed back from whom I'd been before."

Bethany was five years younger than his thirty, full and fair, with modest blue eyes. He courted her, proposed, and the following spring they were married.

They built the house on Powell Street then moved in during the autumn of 1911. It was a steep Queen Anne, asymmetrically Victorian, a doll's house with porch and peaks and shingles. Bethany planted frivolous annuals; Albert raised a brooding hedge of holly.

They were never to have children. Albert more than hints at ambivalence in this regard. The long-awaited pregnancy ended in miscarriage, and Bethany was unable to conceive thereafter. The loss cast a greyness over her -- a shade that stayed with her to the end.

Over in Bosnia, at the end of June, 1914, the Archduke Franz Ferdinand of Austria, along with his wife, was shot to death in his motorcar following an inspection of troops stationed in Sarajevo. The assassin was a disgruntled Serb student, bitter over politics. A few simple bits of lead, a few coughs of smoke and the world went spinning on its way to the Great War.

Woodrow Wilson resisted involvement until German subs took to sinking American ships. Albert enlisted and crossed the Atlantic in 1917, but it was months before he and the other Yanks saw action. He was a medic, of course, which set him in the trenches. He writes of his experiences in his book -- one cannot underestimate the impact the war had on him. I think he found it especially difficult to have so many patients die, but, as he quite bluntly puts it, "the scalpel is no match for bullets."

The worst of it occurred in the smoky, shattered woodlands of the Argonne. Pond likened the horrors there to a slaughterhouse and took home images that replayed in his sleep. One dream would deter him from rest for days on end, even when he returned to the doll's house in Salisbury.

Here is how he describes the dream: "I could not close my eyes that I would not see a great pale face as tall and wide as a sky. It was a young soldier's face, speckled with blood, the thin lips numbly repeating, 'bleeding...bleeding...bleeding...bleeding...'"

As the war was staggering toward its end in 1918, Albert received word of Bethany's death. She had suffered an allergic reaction to a bee sting and died alone, face down in the mums she had been weeding, her throat swollen shut.

Dr. Pond writes: "I have seen the frailty of the human body illustrated with terrifying clarity, and yet mine has survived the dangers of war to pen these words. Despite the bombs and the gas, the cannons, bayonets and rattling Maxims, I sit here whole, while a seemingly innocuous insect, no bigger than a pistol shell, has robbed my Bethany of her life. This is the cruelest of ironies, and it torments me."

I am heading north. It is "day one" and the weather is promising, the mist in the hills burning away to make room for sunlight. The traffic is light this early; my speeding neighbors are mostly large trucks. For once I've made a tasty cup of coffee -- I'll take that as a good omen.

I think of Pond's New England as I drive along Route 9, or "The Pike," as Nana called it. I try picturing the less-congested landscape, the noble structures, the cars of that period. Glimpses of old homes bolster the illusion, but the fantasy is spoiled when I pass the inevitable golden arches and the glimmering seas of consumers' vehicles worshipfully cluttered about titanic malls.

Crows are huddled over something small and dead by the side of the ramp that takes me onto 495. Soon there are only trees to either side and steep perilous cliffs where ledge was blasted to accommodate the road. The highway snakes up through crowded Lowell.

There is a grey sensibility in this city...even in sunlight the bleakness permeates like the ghost of silenced industry weltering in the shadows of abandoned mills.

Albert Pond resumed his medical practice upon returning from Europe, and though he indulged a select number of close friends, his existence was largely solitary, but for the company of a dog. Having had his taste of adventure, he was glad for the uneventful thing that his life had become, relieved to be back in the familiar Queen Anne. Peace of mind, however, remained elusive...

His dreams of war intermingled with nightmares about Bethany's death. He would envision her sitting rigid, creaking in a rocking chair at the foot of his bed, her face a damp mask of crushed flower petals and garden soil, which largely obscured her bloated red features. He was thankful for the obstruction.

Over time the night intrusions became less frequent, the great muttering soldier's face went silent and the compressed semblance of blooms died away like the annuals that once graced the yard.

I can feel my excitement building as I grow closer to my first destination. To think that I will actually be seeing the house where Pond's journey began...how thrilling! I am now leaving the highway, having driven for roughly an hour; I find myself amongst houses and convenience stores, gas stations and other modern-day necessities. Before long I am turning left onto Powell Street and pulling up outside the Queen Anne that Pond built.

I recognize it immediately, for I've seen a photograph of it taken in the mid-eighties for the obscure magazine HAUNTS AND WONDERS, which ran an article on the Pond case. Incidentally, I tried to track down and contact the author of that piece, only to find that he had died in 1993.

The place does indeed look like a doll's house, steep and Victorian, with a front-facing gable, bay windows and a band of patterned shingles that runs above the porch-line. It has changed, of course, the present owners having painted it green with white trim. They also hung window boxes, and sometime between 1920 and now, the dark hedge of holly was removed. Still, I shiver at the sight of the house. This is where it all began.

It was May, according to Dr. Pond's journal, though the seasons might have been misaligned, for the chill spoke more of November, and the sea was the color of ash. Not a religious man, his rituals at that time were comforting repetitions...tea in the morning, the rustling Telegram, a stroll along the shore with his retriever, Rooney.

The beach was empty but for gulls and crows like chess pieces on the sand. The tide was coming in, as were rain clouds. It was the dog that found the naked woman lying in the wet sand. Albert heard the barks and saw the animal in the distance, dancing in agitated half-circles at water's edge. Moving closer, he too saw the body. Incoming waves draped rippling translucence over her legs and lower belly.

She was young and fetching, the hair on her head as dark as the patch below. Her legs were closed and pointing out to the open sea, her arms flung to either side, as if to mock Christ on his cross. The doctor rushed to her side and bent down, first off thinking that she must have drowned -- her coloring suggested as much; she was as pale as the foam that nudged her limp arms. "She appeared so peaceful," Pond wrote, "as if she were merely sleeping."

Before Albert could place a hand on her throat to feel for a pulse, he saw her flattened breasts rise and fall. The hand instead went to her cheek and rested there. "I spoke to her and her eyes opened. Never had I seen such lovely eyes, nor have I since. They were also the darkest eyes that I have ever witnessed."

The woman regarded the stranger without alarm, or any other clearly identifiable expression, for that matter. Pond asked her if she thought that she could move, and she sat up slowly, dripping, her hair running down her throat like ink. He explained to her that he was a doctor and that he was going to take her to safety.

He helped her to her feet and noticed the impression her body had made in the grey sand, an imprint of her graceful back. Waves tripped over each other as they rushed to swallow it.

"I wrapped my coat about her and guided her back to my house, away from the spitting clouds and the sprawling Atlantic. Fortunately there were few other houses between the beach and my dwelling. I was generally up and about before any neighbors stirred, thus, we traveled unwitnessed."

The heavy rain waited until they were secure inside the Queen Anne. It hummed on the roof of the porch and tinkered at the windows. Albert seated the woman on the sofa in his parlor and provided her with towels, but she simply sat there, damp and staring.

The doctor speculated that she was dazed, or perhaps mentally defective, though he tended to doubt the latter. There was a certain something in her eyes, a quality that even he, with his gift for language, was hard pressed to describe. It made him think of the eyes of soldiers back in France, the eyes of those who had seen too much horror, but unlike them, she had made a peace with the horror.

Albert told her his name and asked if she remembered what hers was. She gave no response. He asked if she would allow him to dry her, seeing as she had not made any effort. No response came, so he sat beside her and gently toweled her as best he could. This made him feel awkward.

"Can you tell me anything about yourself? Anything at all? Do you recall anything about how you ended up on the beach? Did someone hurt you? Were you in a boat?"

The visitor remained mute, inscrutable.

"I'd like to examine you, if that would be all right?"

Pond fetched his bag and went about his inspection. The woman was relaxed and compliant and did not even shudder when he placed the cold stethoscope to her bare chest. He did not detect any obvious injury; in fact, she seemed a healthy specimen. Only when he tried to have a look inside her mouth did she react, turning her head away and squinting her eyes. Albert apologized and withdrew.

After the check-up Dr. Pond made tea. He had helped the visitor into his bathrobe and even put a pair of his socks on her feet. They fit loosely, like shedding skin.

"Rather than refer to her exclusively as 'she' and 'the woman' (in my journal) I have decided to call her Arabella," Pond wrote. Further... "Certainly it occurred to me that I should alert the authorities, and I wondered if there were concerned loved ones out searching for this poor lost creature. Still, I made no effort to announce my find. The motivation behind my actions, or lack of action, remains a mystery to me. My intentions were by no means nefarious. I am, after all, a gentleman."

Arabella ignored every form of nourishment offered to her, although she did open the front of her robe, dip a finger into a cup of hot tea, and trace a small circle around her navel.

I step out of the car and take several pictures of the house. I have gone so far as to contact the present owners, explaining that I am retracing the steps of Dr. Albert Pond, but they've shown no interest in allowing me inside the structure. Very disappointing.

It is May now, as it was then, but today the air is warm and bright, and one is tempted to believe that the world is only what we know of it... Streets and homes, jobs, schools, television programs, celebrities, sports, fashions, products, technology, politics and cultures.

Familiar, numbing religions. Science. How easy it would be to be blanketed and blinded by these things, but I refuse that luxury, just as Albert Pond refused it.

The rain had continued into the night. It blew in off the shore and wrapped wet arms around the house. Albert gently urged his guest up the stairs and put her to bed. He covered her and then sat in the rocking chair nearby, watching her sleep -- the dark eyes behind dark lashes, the pale rosebud lips compressed, the winsome face framed in mussed black hair. Perhaps her recall would be improved in the morning, he hoped.

Albert left a candle burning; the hushed light replaced the room with exaggerated shadow. Arabella's face was slack, and her lips parted slightly, the light glimmering softly on her teeth. The doctor remained curious as to why she had averted her head when he had attempted to examine her mouth. He rose up slowly from the creaky rocker and crept closer.

"Ever so carefully I parted her lips with my fingers and there found the most curious anomaly. Her teeth, both upper and lower, were neat rows of small white petrified trilobites."

Trilobites, for those unfamiliar, were prehistoric arthropods that populated the oceans of the Paleozoic Period. Like crabs and insects, they sported exoskeletons, their shape roughly evoking an oval with multiple small legs ranked beneath, as with a horseshoe crab. The bodies were rather flat, segmented, with furrows that divided the back armor into three distinct lobes. Many fossilized examples still exist.

Pond stared until the woman's eyes began to flicker, then he backed away. He paced for what must have been hours, his mind racing, speculating, reaching for the comforting scientific explanation that would not come.

Perhaps she was of North African origin and the fossils were some form of ritual embellishment that had been hammered into her gums. Yes, that seemed reasonable enough, after all, there were various tribes on that continent that indulged in body modification, elongated necks, tattoos, pierced cheeks and nostrils, raised scarring, and lips manipulated to hold decorative disks in place. Maybe some enterprising sideshow entrepreneur was bringing her to America to dazzle audiences -- COME SEE THE FOSSIL-MOUTHED GIRL -- but lost her to the waves and currents.

It still did not seem to add up. If she were in fact from Africa, even the North, or the Middle East, then how could her skin be so uncommonly pale? He had never seen Irish flesh or Scandinavian flesh so white.

Exhausted from pacing, from thinking, and from the long, eventful day, Albert returned to the rocking chair and eventually dozed off.

Dr. Pond dreamt of a rising grey temple, older than the Parthenon, younger than trilobites. It came up through the mist, dripping, dangling slippery black sea-wrack like remnants of a net that failed to confine it. Water gurgled down the stone steps out of the great stone orifice. Moonlight shone within.

He woke in the morning half-light of his chamber and immediately looked to the bed. Arabella was gone, the covers disrupted. Alarmed, the man got up from the noisy rocker and walked out into the hall. He saw that the bathroom door was ajar and his robe, which Arabella had been wearing, was flopped on the floor.

"Hello," he called.

He moved to the door, gave an obligatory knock, then peered in at a startling scene. The woman was reclining in a tub full of water, asleep or dead, her legs open and crooked over opposite sides of the tub. A newborn child, pale as its mother, floated face down and motionless.

Pond dashed to the tub and grabbed the baby out of the water -- both the water and the small body were cold.

He gasped when he flipped the baby over and saw what it had for a face.

To quote his journal: "A seashell was set in place where the child's features ought to have been. It was a scallop shell, evenly ribbed, dull white in color, but for a slight mossy hue. It measured three and a half inches by three and three-eighths inches. The shell was embedded. Flesh framed the outermost edges fastening the mask in place."

The baby was dead, obviously, and while stunned, Pond had the presence of mind to place it on the floor and turn his attention to Arabella. She was alive. Her eyes had opened, and she was watching him impassively. He fired questions at her. Was she all right? Where had the baby come from? Had she left the house to retrieve it from somewhere? Was the baby hers?

She actually nodded in response to the last inquiry.

The man was more than perplexed. While the babe looked newly born, the mother, if she were indeed the mother, had shown no obvious signs of being pregnant. Certainly he'd seen patients whose pregnancies were nearly undetectable to the eye, but they tended to be heavier specimens than this. Besides, there was no blood in the water, no placenta, no umbilical cord.

Albert helped Arabella out of the cold tub, dried her and again put her in his robe before leading her back to bed. She allowed him to examine her, and still there were none of the expected indications that she had given birth.

"I'd like you to remain in bed, if you would," he told her. "Do you understand?"

No response.

Arabella closed her dark eyes. So far she had exhibited no interest in the child. Then again, he had no idea how much time she had spent with it, not knowing when she had vacated the bed. It was possible that she had passed hours with the corpse. Satisfied that she was content to stay put, Pond hurried back to the bathroom, wrapped the baby in a blanket, and took it downstairs to his examination office, placing it on the table.

He weighed, measured and photographed the body. But for the seashell, it was a conventionally formed infant male with a trace of fine dark hair spiraling out from the crown of its head. Eager to see the features beneath the shell, he took up a scalpel and bent in close.

"It made no sense to me how the rim of flesh could have formed around the edges of the shell...it certainly appeared to be a natural growth of skin, but the child would have had to be alive for such a thing to occur. Flesh does not regenerate in the dead, after all. Even upon close inspection I noted no air holes in the shell, so the poor creature would have been suffocated by the mask; again, suffocation equals death, and death precludes skin growth. Had someone stitched the border? Not likely. While I'd once seen a sideshow mermaid which was created by stitching together the upper body of a mummified monkey and the tail end of a dried fish, this phenomenon struck me as genuine."

Pond carefully cut the thin connecting membrane and pried the scallop shell free. He found no features underneath. No eyes, no nose, no mouth, only a circular black hole. The orifice was smooth and bloodless and deep. It was so deep that even with his face pressed to the maw he could see no bottom...no brain, no muscle, no bones.

"Impossible," he said.

Albert took a ruler and lowered it into the darkness. It met no resistance. He took up his flashlight and shone it down, but the darkness stretched farther than the beam. He dropped in a coin and waited for it to hit the end of the tunnel, which it did, eventually, making a soft distant splashing sound.

Normally a steady man, Dr. Pond was trembling when he hurried down to his workshop in the cellar. He tore tins off shelves, scattering nails and tools, fumbling and cursing until at last he found a reel of neglected fishing line and a sinker weight.

Back in the exam room, he stood above the baby with its crater and lowered the line in. "It seemed to go forever," he wrote, "and I was aware of a briny clamminess that rose up against my face."

The line struck bottom at last. Pond marked a point on the line indicating where the opening began and then pulled up the rest and measured it. The hole in the baby's face had a depth of sixty feet.

Pond collapsed in a chair and held his head in his hands. His heart raced at a dizzying rate, and cold sweat beaded his forehead.

In his journal he would note: "Everything that I thought I knew of the world died in that instant. Science shattered, and my sense of reality (which now seemed to me a zeppelin plump with lies) was punctured; it sank to the ground and deflated." He sat there for some time before returning to the thing on the table.

The second time the line was fixed with a hook in the hopes that it might snag something from the bottom -- anything that could offer some explanation, as if any explanation would do. Again the string sank and sank deep into the hollow, but this time something even more startling occurred. Something yanked on the line.

Pond exclaimed and stepped back, dropping the fishing line. He watched as it snaked several feet deeper into the dead baby's face, then slackened. Several moments passed before he collected himself, took it up and dragged it back out. Peering down he saw that something had been attached to the hook.

It was a piece of yellowed paper with words written on it. Wider than the opening in the face of the dead child, the paper had crumpled somewhat on its way out, which, Pond later realized, accounted for the smeared condition of certain freshly scrawled words. The words were still damp and were composed in blood.

The paper might have been torn from a journal, based on its size and texture, and one side was covered in ink-writing that had blurred at some point in its history, most likely from exposure to moisture. That part was entirely unreadable. The back of the page showed the fresh letters, or what was left of them. It read:

FIND FRACTURED (smudged word))
GO TO SUMNER IN (smudged word)
AT LEXINGTON

SIMON BRINK (smudged)

I make the short drive from Powell Street to the humble stretch of beach where Albert Pond discovered the naked woman. I park the car by the road and climb down a steep grassy embankment that hides the sand from the road. The tide is working its way in, the foamy edge stealthy and sensuous, a drowning memory of primordial lace.

Wandering up and down the stretch, I try to picture the scene. This is where he found her. It chills me to imagine. Right here on this very beach, this ordinary-seeming beach.

I take photos of the area, of the cold blue sea, sunny and flashing back at me like paparazzi, and of the pallid grey sand strewn with shells and small stones.

I wonder if Arabella came back here to the Atlantic after she vanished from Pond's Queen Anne? There was nothing to indicate where she went, and the doctor did, in fact, come to this spot when he finally realized that she was not up in his bedroom.

He had spent hours in his office with the dead child, calling down the opening in its head, dangling the fishing line, hoping to snare another clue. But it seemed that the hole, or tunnel, or whatever it may have been, was holding on to its secrets for the time being.

Pond had wrapped the dead thing in blankets and put it in his icebox (to preserve it) before going off to search for Arabella. First he ran down to the shore. Then he climbed into his black 1918 Nash and drove around town, cruising up and down the major roads that led in and out of Salisbury.

He was more than simply concerned about her well-being, though that was certainly a motivation. She was crucial to the mystery that his life had suddenly been inducted into. By nightfall he was growing desperate, and he decided, finally, to go to the police.

The doctor revealed only a minimal amount of information, a description of the missing "patient," to start. He said that he had found her on the beach and speculated that she may have suffered some kind of accident resulting in amnesia. He told them how he had taken her in, how she had slipped off (with nothing but his robe) while he was busy in his office.

Pond was not satisfied with the degree of interest exhibited by the officers he spoke with, and he wondered if he had wasted precious time by even going to the police station. He spent several more hours driving in the dark.

"I had never felt so alone," he wrote. "Never had the universe felt so vast, and I so small within it. I had, through circumstance, been made aware of something, but of what? Something either too horrible or too beautiful for humans to know."

2. THE GEORGIAN INN

A bit of background... I was laid off from my position as a history teacher at the Eastborough Junior High School following a respectable run of eight years. I wasn't alone on the chopping block, however. Some other fine educators were dropped as well. Budget cuts, you know.

Things turned out fairly well, though, and hadn't I been tiring of trying to get the little wretches to learn, or care about something other than video games, dreadful music, fashions, and their insidious little hormones?

I bought a lottery ticket. Don't ask me why, for I've only bought a handful of the things in all my forty-two years. It was a whim, or fate, possibly. At any rate, shortly after I filed for unemployment benefits, I won $500,000. Imagine that.

I bought myself a quaint village colonial over in Grafton and took some time to indulge an interest that my meager teacher's salary had barely allowed me to pursue...the collecting of obscure esoteric books.

The combination of time and money facilitated this secretive passion. I traveled about in search of dusty gems in obscure book shops. I scoured the internet, contacted people who deal in rare volumes and manuscripts. I spent money (I shy at divulging how much!) and quite a bit of energy as well.

Such treasures I found! I came across a copy of *A Book for Pale Eyes*, its cover marked with glistening gilt symbols, and the saturnine grimoire *The Rhyming Goat*, also a (coverless, sorry to say) edition of Justin Pearl's ghostly and evocative *Harvest of Whispers*. I even secured an early ceremonial work by the infamous Brothers Quince -- an untitled circular-shaped book containing odd calligraphy and unsettling pen-and-ink nudes of a dead woman. Curiously, though, the book that made the strongest impression on me was something other than these mystical exercises. It was a battered, unpretentious little thing called *Dr. Pond's Journal*.

I had heard of Pond, of course, having grown up in the same town where he had grown up. I'd heard the titillating local lore from when I was a child. I'd heard about his remarkable deformity, and how he had been accused of murder, and how he had vanished in 1920. But his book, printed by a friend some years after he was gone, was not a book of spells, or medium-conjured communications like *Mrs. Herring's Recipes* (allegedly derived from a skeleton hand -- nailed to a board -- which tapped out Morse code as it received cooking tips from the dead). His was a documentation of a journey into an unknown New England, into an unmapped reality.

Nigel Wagner's small private publishing outfit released a single printing of 1,000 copies of Pond's adventure in 1925. It's become quite a collector's item and sells for several thousand dollars in certain circles. I had made numerous inquiries and finally was directed to a dealer in Vermont who specializes in antique volumes, a man who is rumored to possess such rarities as Marotta's *Book of Awe* and one of three existent copies of *The Coffin-shaped Book*. He had a single copy of the doctor's journal up for sale. I was exuberant when at last I could hold the thing and breathe its smell (like an eviscerated library). It is a slim book, smallish, with plain black covers and moth-colored pages.

Pond's adventure became something of an obsession with me. I spent months trying to track down everything else I could find out about him, contacting people all over the globe, digging for old articles and photographs. I even spoke with a number of folks in Salisbury who had been treated by the doctor, and a woman whom he had delivered. Although she couldn't honestly say that she remembered him, she claimed that she once had a dream in which Doctor Pond (equipped by her imagination with numerous small jointed limbs like a horseshoe crab, or a trilobite) went scurrying down the outer length of her bedroom window in the middle of a blizzard.

Having read and reread Pond's writings, and having done my share of research and investigation, I have set out in the great man's tracks. A great man, you may wonder, how can he be "great" if his name is not in history books, or if his life hasn't been made into a movie (or at least a mini-series)? Well, greatness is subjective, granted, but Pond was an explorer as much as Columbus was.

I lack his courage. I do not intend to delve into the mysteries where he dove freely. I only seek to track and marvel at his footsteps, to document, and to hover at the periphery of what consumed him. Maybe I'm a pathetic creature in this way, but sometimes it is safer merely to follow. I am, in this capacity, little more than a tourist.

There's something about old houses at sunset...they are ghosts made of wood, softening in the dusk that comes upon them like a tide. The Sumner Inn is such a place, sitting there like an enormous brick in the angled light, comforted by the shadows of new green leaves.

The inn, on the outskirts of historic Lexington, was built in 1774. Both ponderous and homey, it is a colonial from the Georgian period, though (ornamentally speaking) a glance informs me that it is not a "High Georgian" -- it lacks the corner quoins, dentil molding and roof balustrade that the more expensive homes of that time boasted.

The clapboards of the house have been painted a sober red, the sort of color it may have sported in its youth, though the early pigment might have been fashioned from crushed bricks. Its symmetry has much to do with its beauty; the door, set beneath a rectangular entablature and a transom window, is positioned in the center, while the nine front-facing windows are evenly spaced. Each window contains twenty-four small panes -- they glow softly, mimicking sunset. The single chimney is an impressive thing, a square cannon trained on Heaven.

I park my car and heft my luggage out of the trunk. The air outside suggests lilacs, while the air inside smells of bergamot. My hostess meets me at the door. She is pleasant, a tall, thin woman. Her dress is decorous, as grey as her hair. She is a youthful seventy, and she moves with an unaffected grace that I had feared was extinct.

Imogene Carlisle and her late husband Steven bought the Sumner Inn back in the early sixties. Fond of history, the pair spent a year restoring the place before opening it to the public. Presently it ranks among the oldest functioning hostelries in the States.

"I feel like I've stepped into the eighteenth century," I say, as I take the tour.

"You have," Imogene says, smiling.

The house has been adorned with antiques and the appropriate colors. The east and west parlors both contain paneled fireplace walls, wainscoting and corner beams. Fine wide-plank pine floors are found throughout. The house virtually hums with history -- I expect to round a corner and come face to face with a man in a powdered wig, or a woman in a polonaise gown.

The stairs in the entry are unconventionally steep and offer their share of creaks. They lead to an upper hall which leads to my room, which is spacious, with a pencil-post bed and a tall chest of drawers. There is a chair where one could spend an afternoon reading, and a writing desk where one could spend an evening writing. I find myself wishing I were staying more than one night. I had, of course, requested the room that Pond had stayed in.

"It's lovely," I say, "perfect."

The Sumner Inn is more of a bed and breakfast these days, though this distinction detracts from the romance of the place. I prefer to think of it as an inn. Imogene serves me and the other two guests in the dining room. She is quite the cook! I'd stand on my head and whistle Dixie for a good piece of salmon, so the proprietor certainly endears herself to me with her choice of repast. Later, as we all settle over tea in the west parlor with only candles and a twitchy log-fire for light, she mentions that the salmon dish came from *Mrs. Herring's Recipes*. Mrs. Carlisle, it turns out, is an interesting woman, no stranger to the sort of books that I yearn for.

The Franks, a middle-aged couple visiting from California, politely extricate themselves from the room once the conversation turns to ghostly communications and a dead baby with a bottomless face.

Imogene knows a great deal about the inn and has taken a marked interest in those who have lived and visited here. How exciting it is to be in a house where Albert Pond actually slept. Maybe he sat in this very room, in front of this very fireplace.

Visiting and talking with another who is familiar with the Pond case is such a rarity that I am actually agitated, and I want to blurt out a stream of questions. Thankfully, the Earl Grey is soothing, civilized, gives me something other than inquiries to put in my mouth.

Half of Imogene's face transforms into shifting copper, the light of the hearth blaze close. Her eyes are such a pale blue that at times they almost look like they have no pupils. She sips her tea, tells me things, sips some more.

"Some say Pond went mad," she muses, "and that there never was a naked woman on the beach, that he never recovered from the war, let alone losing his dear Bethany."

"Yes, I've heard the shell-shock theory. What do *you* think?"

"Well," Imogene sighs, "he may have been mad, but he was mad in the best way. I find myself *wanting* to believe that his adventures were something more than delusional."

I too had been forced to question the doctor's mental welfare. I suppose that's unavoidable. But, he was always a precise man, from what I've read, and even after the episode with the baby, and Arabella's disappearance, his mind remained sharp and orderly. "They" thought Newton and Columbus were mad, after all.

Our conversation turns to the gory missive that Pond pulled out of the hole in the newborn. Albert had studied the note, determined to make sense of it, despite the unintelligible parts.

The note, you'll remember, said:

FIND FRACTURED (smudged word))
GO TO SUMNER IN (smudged word)
AT LEXINGTON

SIMON BRINK (smudged)

Imogene speaks, "While there was no trace of Arabella, the note, at least, offered him some sense of direction, providing he could decipher it. He went to Lexington and asked around to see if there were a man named Sumner whose last name began with IN. In no time he was directed here (to the Sumner Inn). The note was pointing him to a place, rather than a person."

Logs pop in the firebox and orange sparks drift up the flue like fireflies dressed for Halloween.

"The Inn belonged to The Fairfields at the time. Pond assumed that he had been directed to their inn for some reason or other, so naturally he asked if they knew anyone by the first name Simon (with the last name being Brink, or something that began with Brink). They did not."

So far my hostess is relating things that I already know, though she is telling the tale well. I get the impression that she loves seating her guests in this ancient room and filling their imaginations with tales of the inn's past. Her achromatic eyes disclose a master storyteller's sparkle. My questions must wait, however, for it would be next to cruel for me to interrupt.

Imogene goes on to tell how the Fairfields had adopted a stack of old inn registers when they purchased the place, and how they allowed Pond, who'd rented a room, to pore over them. While it took him hours, Pond finally found the signature of one Simon Brinklow, whom had been a guest of the Sumner Inn on October 28th, 1862.

Imogene still owns the registers and she shows me the one in question. The pages are brittle, a dusty citrine, and they smell like an attic. The signature, while much more composed in style, reminded Pond of the one found scrawled in blood on the note he fished out of the dead baby.

With no internet at his disposal, Pond turned to the local library. His instincts (or, some may speculate, his intuition) paid off. He found a book called *Ghosts that Lie; Disproving the Fashion of Spiritualism*, written by a man named Simon Brinklow, and published by Wales and Rowe of London in 1859.

Pond spent the night reading the book, expecting to find some mention of the Sumner Inn, but no reference existed. *Ghosts that Lie* documented Brinklow's uncovering of cheats who used clever tricks like doctored photographs, fake body parts and pseudo-ectoplasm to bilk people seeking to communicate with loved ones who had died. However, all of the cases the author had catalogued had taken place in Britain.

Pond wrote: "I waited for the inn to offer me some manner of sign to justify my being directed there, but no sign was forthcoming. Had I failed this poor soul Brinklow, or was the explanation for his present predicament, his seeming interment in a realm accessible through a dead infant's face, hidden there in the inn, waiting as if an undiscovered key?"

Finally, after staying three days at the Sumner Inn, a discouraged Pond returned home without experiencing anything like a revelation. Not to say that he was defeated. He searched several other libraries and, in Salem, found a second book by Simon Brinklow. This work, called *The Path by Moonlight, an Investigation into Disbelieved Realms*, published in 1865, was a complete turnaround from *Ghosts that Lie*. Intrigued, Pond went on to find out all that he could about the man who wrote it.

Who was Simon Brinklow? He was a British fellow, a portly and headstrong banker who, in 1855, lost his wife and three daughters in a fire. When he learned of the growing spiritualism craze that was sweeping Europe and America, his grief got the best of him, and he began attending seances and paying large sums to mediums who claimed they could put him in touch with his loved ones.

A disillusioned Brinklow soon came to believe that the masses were being duped by charlatans, as was largely the case. Infuriated, he set out on a personal mission to expose the fakes who preyed on the heartsick (himself included). In 1862 his crusade took him across the Atlantic to New York and Boston. But something ironic happened. While meaning to discredit yet another so-called haunting, Brinklow traveled to Lexington's Sumner Inn, where he had an experience that converted him in a sense, and set him out on an exploration of fantastic mysteries.

Though he still recognized the numerous frauds for what they were, he realized that there was indeed another side of things, an unexplored world here on Earth. He wrote and published his second book, but it was entirely dismissed by the scientific community, scoffed at by the religious legions, and resented by the spiritualists he had spent so much energy debunking. Brinklow vanished in 1870 at the age of fifty-five.

Hours passed there in the Georgian parlor with the fireplace snapping and the candles reducing. A small mantel clock rang twelve.

"Midnight," Imogene said, grinning, "That calls for brandy."

We had been oblivious of the time, trading conjecture. She fetched an ambery bottle and two glasses, and we drank a toast to Dr. Pond, and another to Simon Brinklow.

We talked about the event that had inspired Brinklow's change of heart. He had heard stories about a certain spirit known to pay visit to the Sumner Inn. Fractured Harry, as the spirit was known, had been encountered as far back as 1799. Somewhere in his travels, Simon had learned a way to (allegedly) summon the odd spirit, and he gave it a try.

Brinklow whispered a curious little song into an empty glass bottle, corked it, then took it to a cemetery about a half-mile away from the inn. The burial yard was neglected, crowded with pitched slates and high grass, tangled in the shadow of leafless boughs. He set the bottle down beneath a tree, returned to his room at the inn and waited, expecting nothing more to happen.

Sometime in the late hours the man heard odd rhythmic sounds in the hallway outside his room. It sounded to him as if someone were letting sopping, bunched-up towels fall to the floor, repeatedly. The noises came up to the opposite side of his door and stopped. Then came a faint knock. A very faint knock.

Brinklow opened the door. He describes the visitor in his second book: "It gave me the impression of a ghastly puppet, this queer figure thrown together from odd bits. The head was a tea kettle, steaming at the spout, impossibly balanced on the main body which, in all candor, seemed no more than a man's baggy overcoat with nothing like a frame to support it. Fantastically enough, the legs which propelled the creature were fashioned from mop handles, while the damp, stringy heads of those very mops comprised its feet."

When Fractured Harry wobbled into his room and sat down at the little table, Brinklow determined that *this* ghost -- or whatever it was -- could not be a hoax. "The resultant terror at this realization," Simon wrote, "was complete."

The creature placed its hands on top of the table. They were old gardening gloves of battered grey, and they twitched irregularly, emitted the restless buzzing of what could only be bees. True to rumor, Harry, with no corporeal vehicle to call his own, made do with whatever was on hand.

Despite his shock, the hardy investigator maintained composure. The visitor leaned its warm kettle head toward him and a voice hissed out of the steam.

"The words which were spoken by the specter defied the conventions of communication. Certainly they were words, but as for what language, I cannot be bound to say. Thus, I remain incapable of repeating them. Indeed, they were strange to me in the instant that I heard them, and yet, their meaning was without ambiguity. They directed me to a particular location, that and nothing more."

Pond recognized that this passage from Brinklow's second book was informing him about what the first line of the scrawled Brinklow note was about...FIND FRACTURED...no doubt Fractured Harry. Without hesitation, the doctor returned to the inn and, following Brinklow's instructions, performed the conjuration.

Fractured Harry, so local lore would have us believe, appears to everyone in a different form. The figure that Brinklow encountered, for instance, was quite different from what came knocking when Pond did the summoning.

The head was an inverted milk bottle containing a strobing number of fireflies (a bit early in the season for them, but Harry had procured some nonetheless). In this instance, Fractured Harrietta might have served as a better title, for the peculiar conglomeration of items featured a woman's pale slip slunk over a guitar, which gave the figure a shapely cast. A coat hanger mocked shoulders, birch branches passed for arms, and the legs were walking canes with a base of winter boots.

Harry clomped jerkily into the room. Pond stepped back hastily to make room for its entry. A rushing mix of terror and wonder momentarily derailed his ability to think, or as he puts it...

"I could do no more than stand and stare as this impossible figure closed the distance between us, its encased green eyes winking their luminosity, fidgeting in the glass skull."

Then, above the sound of insects clicking against glass, came a series of wispy words. While the language was foreign to the ear, Dr. Pond understood. Fractured Harry, before limping out of the room, down the inn's steep stairs and to who-knows-where, told the man to "Go to the house of Arcangelo Banchini."

Is it any wonder I find it hard to sleep, lying here in the old Georgian room where Pond, and perhaps Brinklow before him, slept? I reflect on my delightful visit with Imogene, and how I am inspired more than ever.

Following our brandies, she had asked if I had any intention of trying the ritual to contact Fractured Harry. She herself had never attempted it, and I told her, "Oh, no...I'm happy just to sit in the bleachers, thank you."

I have now left the Sumner Inn for my next destination, though I have made a brief stop at a small overgrown cemetery a short distance down the road. The grave markers are thin slates, tilted, tired from standing so long. Some bare simple portraits and winged heads produced by colonial carvers, others offer the urn and willow motif. None mention anyone named Harry. There are bottles in the high grass, but they are beer bottles, and it's doubtful that they were used to conjure anything other than inebriation. I take photos of the site, then head on my way.

3. A VISIT FROM WAKEFIELD

Following the encounter with Fractured Harry, Pond discovered something distressing. Upon returning to his house in Salisbury, he opened the icebox to check on the condition of the dead baby and found that the body had reduced to a resinous mass.

"It was completely irregular, so far as decomposition goes. The body seemed to be melting, rather than rotting. While still roughly shaped like a human, the consistency was something else entirely. It was slick and brown and translucent -- the translucency revealing neither organs nor bones. In fact, part of it stuck to the door of the ice box and stretched like taffy when that compartment was opened."

This turn of events forced Dr. Pond to do something that he had thus far resisted. He told someone else about Arabella and the baby. He telephoned his good friend Nigel Wagner (who would later go on to publish *Dr. Pond's Journal*) and shared all. He knew he could trust Wagner, and someone other than himself *had* to witness the baby, for the only proof of its existence, besides his words, were the photographs that he had taken, and some would disregard those, if he ever chose to make public his strange experiences.

Nigel suggested that a third party be allowed to view the child, someone who might be sympathetic to such mysteries. He suggested Professor Earl Wakefield of Pawtucket University in Rhode Island. Wagner had read a paper called *Overlaps*, written by Wakefield, which had to do with the theory that other dimensions existed alongside our own. Further, Wakefield put forth the proposition that there were spots where various dimensions actually overlapped each other, some being natural formations, and others which were *created*. Nigel speculated that the baby was a corporeal overlap.

"In my desperation, I agreed," wrote Pond.

"Despite the fact that the icebox was maintaining its cold, the condition of the corpse appeared to be worsening by the hour," Pond noted. "By the time Nigel arrived in the evening, it was growing softer and darker, and the stench had gotten noticeably worse. I cursed myself, for any chance of performing an autopsy had long passed."

Shortly after ten o'clock that night a car rattled up and coughed outside the Queen Anne. A tall, wiry silhouette moved jauntily along the walk, but there was a pause before the men waiting inside heard a knock. When they opened the door the old professor stood there grinning, sniffing a sprig of lily-of-the-valley that he had plucked from the yard.

"I hope you don't mind," the fellow said. "It's my favorite. Is there any other scent so sweet?"

Wakefield was a horsy-faced creature with a red tempest of hair and ill-fitting spectacles. He was well dressed in a suit and bowtie. He stuck the sprig, with its delicate blooms like tiny white bells, into the buttonhole of his jacket and strode in.

Albert introduced himself and Nigel Wagner. The professor stooped to put his face close to Pond's (Albert had been warned that the professor was an eccentric sort) and remarked, "You were in the war. Only men who were in the war have eyes like *that*."

The three went into Pond's examination office, where the icebox crouched against a wall. There were shelves lined with jars, file cabinets piled with manuals, and the expected tools of the trade. The professor paused to study the eye chart, both with and without his spectacles.

Wakefield exhibited an enthusiasm and sprightliness that defied his age. He lit a pipe and paced while asking Pond some preliminary questions before viewing the baby. He wanted to hear more about Arabella, the birth and the note from Simon Brinklow. Fascinated by the responses, Wakefield mentioned that he too had experienced the wonders of an overlap point.

"Twelve years ago I received communications from a Wampanoag Indian woman. The overlap in that case was a two-foot-wide circle in the center of a pond over in Plymouth."

Albert was eager to hear more about Wakefield's story, and the man's speculations about the nature of these other dimensions, but he knew that the baby was deteriorating by the minute and so he urged the professor to have a look.

"Yes, yes -- let's have a look, why don't we?" Wakefield said, turning to the ice box. He rubbed his hands together, knelt down in front of the thing and handed his glasses up to Pond. "Would you hold these a moment, my boy?"

Wakefield opened the door and peered in. "Oh, my..." he breathed, "Amazing! look how it's-"

The professor reeled back, his scream muffled by a mask of gummy black. What was left of the dead child -- little more than a glistening black cannonball -- had fastened itself to him. His arms flailed as he struggled to his feet and staggered blindly across the room. The other two men rushed to his aid, but all they could do was to cling to his thrashing arms as the dark mass on his face flattened, then shaped itself into a lumpy approximation of features. Steam was seeping out from under the muck and one could hear hissing, as if something were being seared.

A voice other than the professor's came bellowing out of the newly formed face -- it was guttural, garbled as it repeated a single phrase over and over. "Six oceans...six oceans...six oceans..."

The black substance rearranged itself further, taking on a loosely ovular shape with rib-like striations that, for a moment, made it look like an obsidian trilobite. Then, it melted straight into the center of Professor Wakefield's face. The two men who had tried to help him suddenly backed away.

The penetrating mass shaped a vacuous, smoothbore crater. Pond was close enough to get a look into the hole which, he would assert in his journal, appeared to reach deeper than the circumference of a human head would allow.

"All at once a great sucking wind took up," Pond wrote. "Papers flew to the hole, books were drawn violently to it and swallowed, even myself and Nigel had to fight against the force of the vacuum."

The professor had ceased his flailing at this point, and took several resolute steps toward the other men. Wagner managed to get a hold of the door frame and called for Pond to follow, but Pond was determined to remain. He pawed at his shelves even as their bottles flew off and disappeared into Wakefield's face.

The gangly figure stepped closer and closer to Pond, thrusting its orifice forward. It was a horrid sight, bending down as if to kiss Albert, its wild red hair dancing in the wind. The blaring vacuum increased its intensity and Pond started to slide across the floor toward it.

Wagner saw Pond's hands come up -- one let go of a small open bottle of ether, the other a lit cigarette lighter. Both items were drawn into the hollow.

There was a flash and a thunderous roar that could not have simply come from a small bottle of ignited ether. Professor Wakefield was tossed in one direction, Pond in the other. Nigel grabbed his friend and pulled him to safety as the examination room was suffused with flame.

Appalling screams came from the burning chamber, a multitude of voices echoing away as if Pond and Wagner were listening to a string of mountain climbers falling into a cavernous chasm.

Firemen arrived in time to save the Queen Anne, although the examination room and part of Pond's study were destroyed. Professor Wakefield's charred remains were dragged from the rubble; they had been obliterated from the neck up. All traces of the enigmatic infant's body were lost, as were most of the photographs that Pond had taken of it. The only one that remained was burnt along one side so that the seashell-face was no longer visible.

Nana was a collector as well as a naturalist. When she died the attic of her house was filled with treasures stored in boxes of yellowed cardboard. There were shed snake skins like coils of brittle brown lace, shriveled horse chestnuts that once were dark and polished as mahogany; there were stones and pine cones and dead insects she had found and delicately interred in beds formed from cotton balls. These things were as valuable to her as jewelry might be to another.

There were shells, of course, all manner of shells. They were scalloped and spiraled, smooth, textured, colorful and dark. She even had a pair of ponderous conches with shiny pink mouths and pale petrified horns. They were like the skulls of demons or some unclassifiable prehistoric thing.

On the subject of shells... Dr. Pond writes of the shell that he removed from the child. "While the remains of the infant were lost, I was thankful that the shell had survived unscathed. It was safe in my jacket pocket, where it remained at all times. At least I could claim that as tangible evidence.

"I must admit that I had not fully contemplated the potential dangers that might be involved in the kind of exploration I was about. Frankly, I was not even sure just what my purpose was. Proof, in a number of astonishing forms, had forced me onto a road that might take me anywhere.

"On the eve of my leaving, I was tempted to turn away and try to pretend that things were only what I once knew them to be, but it was much too late for that. How could I deny what I had experienced? It was all real; Arabella, the infant, the note from Brinklow, Fractured Harry, and poor Wakefield's demise. To say nothing of the mysterious hollows I had seen in not one, but two human heads.

"I spent that night at Nigel Wagner's home, where I was plagued by strange dreams. Mind you, I had seen atrocities in the Argonne, but the professor's violent end disquieted me to my core. In my sleep I imagined him with that wide open darkness where his features had been.

"Another troubling image was that of the pulpy mass that seemed to mock a face as it covered that of the old gent. In my slumber it loomed like a sky, and I heard it repeating that particular phrase again and again. 'Six oceans...' Whatever could it have meant by that? Previously I had seen a photographic portrait of Simon Brinklow. Only in retrospect did I liken his image to that dark one that took shape and spoke.

"In the morning, following tea and Telegram, I thanked Nigel for all his help, and because he agreed to tend my dog Rooney in my absence. Not one for tears, I made an exception as I bade farewell to my two dearest friends. I shook the man's hand and then bent down so that the dog could give me his paw."

4. STRANGE APPARATUS

I am alone on the open road. We've all imagined the archetypal highway stretching off into a distance of uncharted possibilities -- a dream that both thrills and frightens. But, I am spared the brunt of those sensations, for I am only an admirer of explorers, and I'm traveling to a specified destination. Others have done the dirty work, so to speak, in this case. Still, the solitude suits me, and the sky is such a wide morning blue above the shadow-mottled pines that I delight in the illusion that I too am an adventurer.

I cross the border, and a large sign welcomes me to New Hampshire, The Granite State. I proceed to Manchester, where the prime thoroughfare is long and wide, stretching toward garages and unglamorous localities in one direction, while the other ends with noble old houses smacking of money. There is something earnest about this city, a working-class lack of pretentiousness that an old mill town ought to convey. I am spared the studied hipness of say, Boston's Newbury Street, and the glare of icy glass skyscrapers. Instead, there is brick and verdigris and weathered steeples poking above the neighborhoods.

It is a Sunday morning, and the traffic is light. My instructions guide me without incident to a residential area dominated by Victorians. I recognize the house that I am looking for, park my vehicle and shoot several pictures. The light-grey building rises steeply from the street, so it is a short walk to the impressive double doors.

This is the Arcangelo Banchini House. Built in 1878, it is an imposing example of Italianate architecture. The roof is almost flat, with eaves that project out, supported by ornamental brackets. There are bay windows -- both upper and lower story -- on one side; the rest are long thin things with arched brows. While the facade boasts a fine entry porch, the most dramatic feature is the narrow tower that presides above. Each of its four sides holds a pair of hooded windows beneath a precipitous mansard roof that sits atop like a strange angular hat.

Simon Brinklow had already vanished by the time this place was erected, but Albert Pond certainly paid visit here. It was in the summer of 1920. This is where Fractured Harry had directed him.

I have an appointment with the present owner, the great-grandson of the brilliant inventor who built the house. Vincent Banchini answers the door in a plaid bathrobe. He has a coffee mug in hand and a cigarette hanging from the corner of his mouth. Funny how we envision people we've met over the telephone differently from how they turn out to be in the flesh. This man is not what my imagination had made him out to be. He is a middle-aged fellow of average proportions, balding on top, with a longish black tail tied in back. He is unshaven and wears round sunglasses the color of stout.

"Man," he says, "you're punctual." Then he laughs, vigorously shakes my hand, and drags me in before releasing it.

I'm immediately ushered into a sunny parlor full of heavy Victorian furniture. A figure hovers by a tea table dressed in a sack-like Middle Eastern burka. The dark garment covers the wearer from head to foot, but for a thin meshed opening at the eyes.

"This is Tabina, my housemaid," Vincent says with a gesture. Then, close to my ear, he confides with a snicker, "I like a challenge when I mentally undress a woman."

I struggle out a little laugh and bid good morning to the inscrutable female pillar.

My host feels the urge to clarify: "Don't get the wrong idea. I'm not some subjugating patriarchal control freak. She chooses to dress this way. It's her traditional garb, as they say."

"Yes, of course," I return.

Vincent thrusts a finger at me and blurts, "Coffee! Don't tell me...cream and two sugars."

"That's right," I say.

The man beams. "I can always tell. I have a sense for these things. With tea I'm a little foggy, but coffee drinkers, I can read 'em a mile away."

We sit. Tabina pours and prepares my coffee. She does a better job than I am known to do.

"I'm also a human thermometer," Vincent chatters. He sticks an open hand into the air, thinks a moment, then proclaims, "Sixty-six degrees. Guaranteed." Then he scrunches out his cigarette and lights another.

The draped figure, like an upright body bag, stands solemnly a few paces from the table. I find this intimidating. Considering the locale, how can I know for certain that there is even a human under that thing?

Vincent carries the conversation. "So, you're traipsing around in the tracks of that Pond guy, eh? Cool. I can't honestly say I know much about him. Hey, didn't he kill somebody?"

Before I can answer, Vincent is up on his feet and rushing across the room. He plucks an oversized book off the cushion of a sofa and returns, puffing a trail from the cigarette in his mouth.

"See," he says, "here's his signature."

There, indeed, is Dr. Albert Pond's mark. The old leather ledger contains nothing but signatures, the names of those who experienced the wonders of the hidden room below this structure.

"My great-grandfather didn't believe in documentation. He never wrote any articles about his work, no books, nothing. Not even a journal. He kept it all up here..." He taps his head. "His work was too important, too secretive, and he didn't want it falling into hands that would have misused it, and there are always plenty of those around. Undesirable hands. He kept his secrets to himself and worthy associates."

"Understandably," I utter.

"So, this book of signatures, and the contraption itself, are all that remain."

Vincent allows me to photograph the ledger. Before I can finish my coffee, I am being led down a steep wooden staircase into the under-chambers of the old house. There is a short dark hall with an adjacent compartment dominated by a coal bin and some kind of boxy object that looks to be a furnace of sorts. At the end of the hall there is a heavy rust-colored door constructed entirely of metal. The host opens it.

"Here we are," Vincent announces, "the *Spirito Macchina*, as old Arcangelo called it."

Vincent Banchini is a metal sculptor, a vocation undoubtedly inspired by his great-grandfather, whose artistry produced the dimly lit room we enter. There is nothing extraordinary about the shape of the enclosure. It is a simple rectangle. This rectangle, however, contains a petrified jungle of baroque clutter, the walls and ceiling textured with rusty mechanical detail, the lines of which bear an archaic and ornamental grace -- the Victorian impulse for embellishment evident. There are crusted pipes and leather bellows, flaking gears and oily pistons, chains, springs, grates, all delicately smothered in dusty webs. The room is a machine.

A single high-backed chair stands on a low platform facing away from the entry. It looks upon a pair of tall narrow doors that are streaked with what I hope is only rust. Void of knobs, handles and even hinges, they are set into the far wall.

"It's amazing," I breathe.

"Still works, too," my host notes nonchalantly.

"Really?" He had not mentioned that on the phone when I had arranged to come and photograph the apparatus.

"Sure. Last week I saw this cute little brunette with no arms or legs, just an umbilical cord whipping around like a drunken cobra."

I get a chill.

"Here, hop in the pilot's seat," Vincent says, a fresh cigarette bobbing.

I stare at him. "Do you mean you want me to *operate* it?"

"You didn't drive all this way just for a few snapshots, did you?" He peers over his glasses.

The fact is I'm more than happy just snapping my pictures. "Thank you, Vincent, but I'm fine."

He looks hurt. "Oh, come on, don't be a pussy. This is an opportunity to look beyond the Big Lie. Give it a shot."

I've never been good at saying no. My students had taken terrible advantage of that weakness. Before I can find the words to rationalize a refusal, I am sitting in the stiff metal chair.

Vincent blathers, "I've had all types of things come through here, and they're not all people who've died. I had a Swiss mountain climber who disappeared in the Himalayas back in 1938. Guy hadn't aged a day. He stayed out *here*, by the way, ended up going back to the home country."

I suddenly feel feverish.

But there's more: "I've even seen some things that aren't quite human, but the beauty of it is that you can sort of window shop. If you see something coming through that you think is bad news, you can throw a lever and bingo! It gets shut out."

I actually stammer, "I'm not sure I--"

"Okay, here's how it works...

"If you're looking to talk with someone specific, you call to them through this thing." He points to a funnel, a refurbished ear-trumpet maybe, that hangs to the left, at face level. It is the terminal end of a twisty metal pipe that snakes up into the ceiling.

The man goes on, rapidly instructing me on the use of several tall levers that jut up from the floor at the base of the chair.

Ashes rain down Vincent's bathrobe as he looks at me squarely and warns, "Remember, if you see the right door opening, it means you've got something undesirable trying to come through. Don't hesitate, just go for your lever."

"But...."

Vincent is heading for the door. "It won't work if there's more than one person in the room, but don't worry -- I'll be right outside. Okay, I'm off to fire this baby up..."

The door behind me clangs shut and I find myself sitting here alone in a haze of cigarette smoke with my camera in my lap like a bulletless gun. I feel as if I am sitting in a submarine, deep in a night-dark sea. It may as well be night for the darkness of the chamber, the meager light sources vague, set somewhere in the jumbled components.

I find myself questioning the degree of belief that I have in all things supernatural. At a safe distance, I would have thrilled at the *thought* of an opportunity to have actual contact with Pond, but now, seated in the darkness beneath the Banchini House, I feel only trepidation. Maybe Pond was indeed a madman, maybe there never was an Arabella, or a baby with a seashell face, or overlaps where dimensions merge. Maybe this room is an entertainment, or a fake, like doctored Victorian "ghost" photographs, mock ectoplasm, profitable spirit-knockings and the like. Maybe Vincent is rushing into a hidden room to operate levitating bed sheets, or to moan and rattle chains through one of the vents. Maybe his great-grandfather Arcangelo Banchini made his fortune hoaxing during the spiritualist craze.

Trembling, I hear a soft hiss of steam as the lights flutter. A gear alongside one of the walls squeals and starts to revolve, hesitantly at first, loosened scabs of rust clicking like hail as they fall to the metal floor. Then plates in the floor begin to rumble as mechanisms beneath the room stagger to life, groaning and rasping. I hadn't realized that there was another level *beneath* the cellar. As the platform under my feet vibrates I find myself hoping that the plates are stable and that I don't end up falling through the floor, chair and all. To my left something bangs as though someone has hurled a hammer. Pistons pulse, and the whole chamber rattles like a factory. There is clanking and squeaking, and I imagine disrupted mice scurrying unseen over the floor, their footfalls lost in the cacophony.

"What if this is *real*?" I say to myself.

I must do something. If spirits, or whatever, are being conjured, it's best that I dictate what they are. I turn to the mouth-funnel and stutter...

"Albert Pond...Dr. Albert Pond..."

I hear several loud booms as if something powerful is punching to get through the metal doors.

"Albert Pond, please...Albert Pond...."

Pale motion draws my eye. Only a mist of steam leaking from a pipe. But then a more dramatic movement. One of the far doors is starting to open.

It is the right door sliding up into the ceiling like a guillotine blade in reverse. I tense, recalling what Vincent had said about the right door. Something bad is trying to enter.

I look down at the stiff levers. He had jabbered instructions about what to do if the bad door opened. But there are three levers, and he was talking so fast that I didn't quite take in what he was saying. Which lever do I pull?

The door makes a grinding sound as it goes up. I see only darkness beyond it. The door is fully open. My eyes adjust, and the light reveals a vague figure seated in a chair. It is thin and dark, coming into focus as the chair slides forward on rails. The chair jerks as it halts and the ghastly metal puppet sitting there lurches forward.

I cry out and grip the arms of my chair.

"Dear God!"

It's an animatron and nothing more, I tell myself, like the figures at Disneyland. Its lines date it as a work of the Victorian mind, for like the other machine parts that surround me, it has grace and floridity, the elegance of a past sensibility. But I am too frightened to be awed by the technological aspect.

The puppet has a demon face, part man, part beast, the prominent snout revealing upper and lower sets of sharp black teeth as the mouth opens, and the thing jerkily stands up from its chair, joints whining.

"*Expletive!*"

I look back at the levers, struggling to remember. What if I were to try them all?

I get a better view of the torso now. It is split down the middle and has lines suggesting ribs, or the definition on the shell of a trilobite. The thin arms bend at the elbow, and skeletal hands reach to open the twin plates of the chest as if a big black book.

Now I am looking into a window of dull luminescence. Mist in moonlight, or a low-wattage light bulb drowning in milk. My eyes try to adjust, or make out detail, but the light is like water, shifting, protective of its secrets.

I lunge for one of the levers and yank it toward myself. Nothing happens.

I begin to notice nebulous spheres rising like great bubbles in the water-light. They bob, floating closer to the window in the metal demon's chest.

I must try another lever... Something is coming.

They are faces, I can see that now as they hover closer, eagerly jockeying for escape. The chamber around me is clanging and banging, the gears rotating, the pistons stomping like the feet of Frankenstein's creation.

Are the faces only partly formed, or is it the sickly glow of their interring space that keeps them indistinct? They are mournful things, no matter, the eyes smudged or bandaged, the woeful mouths biting at the air. One moves closer to the window than the rest, and a thin arm slides out and paws at the steam that is now blurring the dark room.

I dive forward and pull both remaining levers at once. One is stuck, rusted and resistant, but I persist, and they both slide toward me at last.

The entire room jolts -- a hurtling vehicle impacting against something stationary. The lights flicker and fade, but I see a trace of movement before they are blinded entirely. The puppet figure flops back down in its seat, the book-like chest closing as the chair retracts into blackness, emitting a shrill metallic screech.

I find myself in total darkness, and, after a few clinks and rattles, in silence.

"You broke it!" Vincent Banchini screeches like a little girl when he enters the Spirit Machine.

Steam in the air accentuates the beam of his flashlight as it sweeps about the room. Next, it is blazing in my face and I am being interrogated.

"What did you do?"

I can hardly think at this time. I point at the levers.

"The bad door opened -- there were faces -- something was climbing out -- I pulled one lever but nothing happened, so I pulled the other two."

"Simultaneously?" Vincent's voice remains high as if he has been enraged into a second puberty.

I nod, and the man covers his face with a hand and groans. When he drops his hand he swivels and aims the light at the right door.

"Nothing got out, I hope?"

"I don't think so. The metal figure retracted, and the door shut."

Vincent skulks about the room and peers into the clutter of components, looks up and down and behind things. I apologize repeatedly, but the man is too busy muttering to himself to take note.

"Thousands," he's saying, "it will cost me thousands to fix this thing."

I find my way to the door and step out into the little hall. Such a relief to be out of that room! Vincent exits right behind me and calls over my shoulder, "Tabina!"

The being in the burka appears presently. Vincent has replaced his flashlight with a cigarette. He gestures with it.

"Show this man the door."

This is a dreadful motel room, but it suits my mood. I almost embrace it as a punishment, though I'm afraid to touch anything lest I catch some dreaded disease. The crooked pictures are uglier for their crookedness, and the pulsing music from the adjacent chamber reflects the baseness and lack of aesthetics that typifies this modern culture, despite its glorious technological sophistication. (Ironic how we seem to be becoming a more stupid lot as our technology advances...perhaps, in some way, *it* is culpable).

I am confused and disheartened. I honestly don't know what to make of my experience at the Banchini House. While I am stung by Vincent's rage, I am also angry with him for coercing me to try out the machine after I had made it clear that I did not want to. Certainly I'm guilty for causing injury to a unique piece of Victorian technology, or, worse yet, a metaphysical device.

But is it really the mystical machine that it is made out to be? Pond believed it was, and didn't his experience bear out that opinion? How can I distinguish whether the things I saw were more than a magician's stunt? What did I *really* see? Was there a hidden projector painting faces on the steam?

More irony...for one who had set out to retrace a trail of supernatural exploration, the thought that keeps me from falling asleep is this... What if the things I saw were indeed real? And on that note, what if I did not shut the machine down in time to stop that ghastly creature from getting out into this realm?

5. BRINKLOW'S DISAPPEARANCE

Eunice Rice was despairing over her failing memory. She could scarcely remember where she set down a teacup, yet her childhood days returned to mind vividly, exhuming the colors and sensations of the village that had been home; wild August fields buttered with goldenrod, meteors spitting across the cold night sky, ponies and dizzy dragonflies, a restless puppet of unpainted wood, and an old woman who lived under the ice of Beeton's Pond and chewed at it with her horrible teeth.

Now, Eunice was an old woman, and with her memory what it was, she could not say for certain *where* the haunted bushel basket had come from. In the final pages of his journal, Simon Brinklow wrote of Eunice Rice and her preoccupation with her failing memory. And he wrote of a weathered, innocuous-looking basket filled with leaves.

It was November of 1870 when he made the hilly trip from Massachusetts to the Rice homestead, situated on the outskirts of Shaftsbury, Vermont. Nearly eight years had passed since Brinklow had gone from passionate defrauder to one dedicated to supernatural exploration. His book *The Path by Moonlight* had been published (and scoffed at) by the time he had returned to America to pay a second visit to Fractured Harry.

Settled in his room, Brinklow repeated the conjuration. He whispered the little song into a bottle, then left that in the lonely cemetery down the way from the Sumner Inn at Lexington.

Harry, as before, came to his room, but this time he had a water bucket for a head. It was a sturdy thing of oak staves bound with bands of hoop iron. Two apples, like bulging red eyes, were held to the bucket by long rusty nails. His torso was a man's white shirt, rustling with autumn leaves and mice, while the legs were twisty branches of birch. This time Harry stepped very gently, for his feet were ornate preserve jars from India.

When Brinklow had previously encountered this spirit, it had communicated a destination to him. He had gone to that place, of course, and from there ventured to another location of enigmatic significance. And on and on. Each place he visited seemed to be a stepping-stone bringing him closer to some great mystery.

In his journeys, Simon had encountered things so terrifying that he hesitated to describe them, but he had also found undocumented beauty that language could not hope to convey.

The man spent years traveling from place to place until he came to something of a dead end. It occurred to him that he might find direction from Harry, so he crossed the grey Atlantic, to the very spot where his adventure had begun.

Once again Harry, in wispy words that were not words, described a place. An old farm in Vermont, and a Gate of Leaves. In the morning, Brinklow packed his things and headed north.

The sky above Vermont was like an unfinished painting of the sea, the man noted in his journal, marking his arrival at the Rice farm. It was a stormless grey awaiting an artist's brush to add the detail of waves.

Brinklow took great interest in Eunice's childhood tales about the strange puppet, and the lady in the pond, but he was most eager to see the unusual basket which had the town abuzz.

It looked like any bushel barrel of its day, but for the fact that it was full of dry leaves, their bright October colors faded to browns and muted salmon. As for it being haunted, Brinklow had his own thoughts on the matter, based on what he had heard.

A few examples: A chicken, tossed into the leaves in the basket, did not come back out. A pitchfork poked into the thing found no bottom. The container gave things as well took them. Eunice claimed that small coppery fish flew out of the leaves on several occasions. When dropped they shattered like glass. But, when tossed up into a night sky, the glimmering fish would hang in the dark like stars.

On the 15th of November, 1870, Brinklow wrote: "The barrel appears not uncommon in any way. While it is weathered, I am not given the impression that it is a thing of great antiquity. The bands encircling the upright slats of wood are rusted, but sturdy enough. Likewise, the leaves within are ordinary to the eye, though I detect a subtle scent that reminds me of brine."

Shortly after making that final notation, the man began a tactile examination of the bushel basket. He tapped at the sides with a penknife, then with a brave little smile reached his hand down into the leaves.

Brinklow could find no bottom, though his arm was long enough that he should have. He thought he felt small slippery things brush across the top of his hand -- fish perhaps, swimming in the leaves. Then, he reported to the few witnesses present that he felt hair. Long, silken hair that might belong to a woman.

The man tried to grasp the hair, but it slid from his fingers and hissed elusively through the leaves. He reached deeper, leaning over the edge of the creaking basket, groping until most of one arm was submerged. Again he got hold of the long slinky hair, grabbing onto it like reins, even as he felt something taking hold of him. A sinuous pressure coiled about his arm. He said it felt like a constricting snake.

Whatever it was, it dragged him headfirst into the rasping barrel. Onlookers, standing a safe distance away, could not get to the man in time. They were stunned by the speed of his abduction. One moment he was there kneeling by the barrel, the next his feet were sticking straight up out of the leaves, his portly form impossibly swallowed before their eyes.

6. DR. POND AND THE SPIRITO MACCHINA

I am rereading the section in Albert Pond's journal where he visits the dark, clanging room beneath the towering Italianate house in Manchester, trying to see if his experience will give some perspective to mine.

Pond, like Simon Brinklow before him, had embarked on a strange path of stepping-stones. His experience began with the discovery of Arabella, and (to recap) continued with the shell-faced baby, Brinklow's note, the discovery of Brinklow's books, the melting of the infant, the strange and hideous death of Professor Wakefield (who wrote of the overlap theory) and Fractured Harry, who sent him to the Banchini House in New Hampshire.

Arcangelo Banchini, who built the house and invented the Spirit Machine, was in his seventies when Dr. Pond went to visit him, and while the man's health was failing, his mind remained sharp, and his dark eyes revealed great intensity. Pond wrote that his host was a very serious sort with no time left for humor or idleness. Similarly impatient with small talk, Pond respected the older man's directness.

The machine-chamber was undergoing some modifications at the time; Banchini cautioned Pond that there had been some "difficulties" with it, and that it required some refining. A Belgian fellow, who had traveled a great distance in hopes of contacting his deceased twin sister, had left the room mysteriously deficient in fingers. There were no wounds, nor blood, merely a lack of digits. The man did, incidentally, enjoy a visit with his sibling.

Pond had familiarized himself with the late Professor Wakefield's writings and was intrigued to read, according to the hypothesis put forth, that overlaps might be either natural formations or created. In the case of the Banchini device, the dimensional gateway did not exist in that spot prior to the creation of the machine.

I find it somewhat reassuring that even Pond was apprehensive about taking his next step, so to speak, closing himself in that subterranean chamber amidst the noisy clutter, with the two doors facing him, and the unknown pressed up against the other side of those doors.

Pond wrote of his intentions: "I could not help but feel a kindredness with Brinklow, and something more, a sense of obligation. He had reached out to me with his note, after all. He must certainly have been trapped *somewhere*, in who knows what conditions. Thus, my aim was to attempt to release him, or at the very least to gain some communication with him."

Pond spoke Simon Brinklow's name into the trumpet-like apparatus hanging down to his left. In his journal he did a fine job of evoking the rest of his experience, detailing the dimness and the noise of the many moving parts around him, then the lifting of one of the doors on the other side of the chamber. In his case it was the left door that opened.

"Once the door had retracted fully, I found myself gazing upon a seated figure the size of a grown man. It was gracefully shaped from metal, and rather skeletal, with a chest that made me think of a trilobite in that it was roughly ovular with pronounced ribs nestled against each other."

The chair holding the puppet slid out on its track, and Pond had a better look at its face. While lacking any distinct expression, the bland suggestion of human features somehow displayed a kind of tranquility.

The puppet stood up, and artificial hands reached to open the hinged plates of the chest. Pond found himself facing a soft luminosity that filled the opened area of the torso, like a window misted by moonlight and breath. After several moments he discerned movement there in the watery light -- a shape was moving toward the opening, when suddenly the entire room rumbled painfully.

Pond grasped the arms of the chair as the puppet flopped back into its seat, rattling like a suit of armor. The sides of the chest compartment clanked open and shut repeatedly, a Cyclops blinking. Then its chair flew back and forth on its rail, backward into the darkness, then out into the only slightly more illuminated area where the man sat. It did this several times, squealing metallically until the sliding door came banging down on top of its head. That was when the room went black and Pond sat there listening as the works shuddered and pinged their way toward silence.

It was at about that time that Pond felt something strike him in the chest, like a fist, and he himself blacked out.

When Albert awoke he was on a sofa in the parlor of the large house, and Arcangelo Banchini was leaning over him, studying him with dark eyes.

Pond had lifted his hands and examined them. "Well," he'd said, "I appear to have all my fingers."

Banchini was profusely apologetic, like a man whose prized dog has bitten a guest on the leg. It was clear that his pride was wounded, because his invention had malfunctioned. Pond was gracious nonetheless, and expressed interest in returning for a second try as soon as the machine was up and running again. He had gotten a titillating glimpse, and that, he assured his host, had made the trip worthwhile.

As for the blow to his chest, there was no mark to be found, no bruising, no redness, no injury that could be seen, although in his journal Pond would confide that the area just above his solar plexus felt both sore and tingly.

7. SEPTEMBER

I must be going mad; there can be no other explanation. Days have passed since I have been able to sleep. All I do is pace my rooms and peek out around the shades. Maybe I need to talk to a therapist -- maybe I'm suffering some sort of anxiety disorder. I've probably spent too many years reading strange old books.

Following the upsetting incident at the Banchini House, I decided to postpone the rest of my adventure indefinitely. It was a sad thing, admittedly, and I've admonished myself over it, abandoning the dream that I had waited years to pursue. But something happened in that dark underchamber, something that frightened me deeply, and so I made the painful decision to return home.

I know it's foolish. In fact, nothing notably alarming occurred until this past Saturday. Every year the Eastborough Library holds a sidewalk book sale, selling off old unloved books for charity. The public is invited to bring boxes of their own to offer as well. Most of the books are works of dreadful fiction, but I've found some diamonds among the coal. Since my return I've been trying to read things other than archaic esoteric texts, so I thought I might give the sale a try.

It was a fine day in the first week of September, blue-skied, bright, with the early leaves turning. There was even a trace of coolness in the air, a great relief, considering the muggy August I had suffered. It was the kind of day that makes me want to eat plain doughnuts and drink hot cider.

Long tables were set up on the sidewalk along West Main Street; others crowded the front lawn in front of the noble old structure of beige stone. I wandered among the tables, quietly scrutinizing their contents. Books were stacked in irregular gravity-defying pillars and stuffed into cardboard boxes, the white splits in worn bindings giving the impression that their titles were emerging through static.

There were a good many potential buyers perusing about, and they seemed nice enough, book-lovers being a more civilized lot. I picked up a slim volume on British war ships of the late 1700s and was standing in the shade of a maple, flipping through its pages, when I felt something cold touching my arm.

Looking down, I noticed a pale hand lighting on the back of my wrist. The wrinkled fingers were slender, with nails that looked like tiny bleached trilobites.

Instinctively I stepped back and looked up to see the face of the person who had touched me. There were leaves tangled in the long white hair which blew across the face -- a shifting mask obscuring all but the toothless smile.

A rush of adrenaline spun me from the stranger. I dropped the book onto the nearest table and found myself walking swiftly away from the crowd and the tables and the cool shade of the library. I crossed West Main -- blood parading through my head with heavy feet -- and did not turn to look back until I had reached my car.

Light flashed on the window of the heavy library door as it swung shut. Leaves trembled down onto heaps of faded books. People milled and hunched over tables. People chatted and smiled and made purchases. The world appeared ordinary -- no sign of the white-haired individual with prehistoric fingers.

I drove straight home, where I have remained since. Sleepless. Pacing. I obsess over the incident, replay it over and over in my mind. Was the hand that touched me as cold as my memory tells me it was? Wasn't it simply some nice little elderly person on the verge of asking some innocuous question? How could someone really have little white trilobites for fingernails?

There must be something wrong with me, acting this way. I think about the Banchini House and what I saw in the opened chest of that metallic demon. But what did I see? Those faces bobbing in the strange light were nothing other than images cast by a hidden projector, weren't they? The one that was reaching out, or pulling itself out, was no more than a clever illusion. That *has* to be the logical explanation. It was a prank, a little something to agitate the imagination.

September whispers around my house, a blend of crickets and breeze. It gets dark earlier now. I prop myself up on coffee legs and pace. I'll have another cup. I hear a noise out in the dusk and go to the window, peel back the edge of the drawn shade and peer out. Only back-lit leaves flitting past the street lamp, straying from their limbs.

8. BOOKS

Burnt sage leaves have left a strange smell throughout my village Colonial, remnants of a protection ritual I performed some hours ago -- a simple spell taken from *Cricket and Moth*, an anonymously written volume that appeared in 1935. The book has no formal title, though the cover bears the moon-colored image of a moth above a silhouetted cricket, both set against a pale green background. The lettering inside is curious; it resembles black ants arranged to form words. The spells themselves are elegant in their simplicity, poetic in essence.

Yes, I've returned to my strange books. I spent hours distracting myself with Nana's volumes on old New England houses, but eventually, inevitably, I went to the bookcase in my study where my collection of rarities resides.

Lying to myself has not worked. I know what I saw at the Banchini House. I actually experienced the cold from that stranger's touch, and I saw the trilobite fingernails with my own eyes. Albert Pond and Simon Brinklow knew that the world is much more than we think it is. I know this too.

So the question now is...what should I do? Something made its way through the overlap in Banchini's machine, and whatever it is, it's followed me all the way from Manchester. Terrifying as that realization is, it serves me no purpose to deny it.

I can't exactly call the police and report a thing like this. But, there must be someone I can turn to -- someone stronger, more capable of confronting danger. I am reading *Dr. Pond's Journal* again. Maybe his courage will bolster me, maybe his experiences will give me some insight into how to proceed...

9. CROCKER'S BITE

The failure of Arcangelo Banchini's Spirit Machine was a setback to Pond. He wasn't sure how next to proceed. He attempted to find out more about the "haunted" apple basket into which Brinklow had vanished, but nothing came of his inquiries. No one seemed to know what had become of the basket, and the Rice Farm had long since fallen to neglect. He wished that he could return to The Sumner Inn and contact Fractured Harry again, but Harry would only come to a particular individual once every seven years.

One rainy evening, cooped up in a brick hotel overlooking a glum tract of Manchester, Pond was surprised by a knocking at his door. It was the desk clerk, reporting that a visitor was asking for him. An old man. Pond told the fellow to send the visitor up.

Albert was glad to see Arcangelo Banchini again. The old man was soaked from the rain, his fedora dripping. Pond invited him in and they sat a while, talking. Banchini offered a gnarled little Italian cigar and Pond shared some illegal brandy (Prohibition had gone into effect back in January).

After apologizing once more, Banchini said, "I've seen many amazing things, my friend. You would think I was mad if I told you. And I have learned remarkable things, because of the machine; I have learned about places that interest men like us. There is one in particular that you might find useful..."

Pond was intrigued, of course.

I am on the road again, an hour and a half away from home, traveling in north central Massachusetts. Route 2 takes me through Templeton, Phillipston, and beyond, on into Erving, where the road curves close to the towering paper mill. White clouds swell from the stacks and the air almost smells like the sea. I drive along the Millers River, through a landscape of wooded hills and enduring bridges. There are cadmium fields of goldenrod, open tracts of farmland, stands selling apples and pumpkins.

I feel somewhat better for being this far from the area where I encountered the white-haired stranger. Still, my relief is tempered, for if it was able to follow me from New Hampshire to central Massachusetts, then I'm not sure I'll be truly safe anywhere.

What does it want with me?

It is late morning and I have entered historic Deerfield, famous for the French and Indian attack of 1704, and now known for its grand street of 18th and early 19th century houses. As much as I would love to stroll among those architectural wonders, beneath the large trees that shade the stretch, I feel that all things pleasant must wait until I have taken some form of action to further defend myself.

Over the years I have been in contact with a good number of interesting people representing a varied range of mystical systems and spiritual bents. Most have come to my attention through my pursuit of collectible books. I know astrologers, psychics, Wiccans, herbalists, dowsers, ceremonial magicians, and on... One of the latter is a young woman named Lauren McAlester who possesses the uncanny ability to track down rare items useful to those practicing the unconventional arts.

Lauren was very sympathetic to my situation when I spoke with her over the phone. She is one of the few humans I know whom I would even have considered relating the experience to, for while my circle of contacts is rather wide, I am a solitary sort, and private by nature. I guess I am like Dr. Pond in that way -- I have more acquaintances than friends.

Turning onto a side road, I come upon a Second Empire house set back behind a diminishing hedge of lilac. A tallish hydrangea stands to one side; at a distance the clustered blooms look like puffs of cotton candy. The house is a small specimen for its type, just two stories high, with the windowed upper level encased in a mansard roof. There is a small entry porch at the left of the facade -- I park my car and head for this.

A thin red-haired woman bounds from the house to greet me. To look at her, one would never suspect that she engages in ritual magic, conjuring arcane forces and the like. She is freckled, with a pleasing plainness, her hair braided behind her. Her clothing is unostentatious -- jeans and T-shirt. I receive a big smile and a hearty handshake; her fingers smell of tomato plants.

Lauren leads me to the back of the house, where the grounds remind me of Nana's garden. There is an English cottage sensibility to the space as opposed to the stiffly manicured look so popular in these times.

We drink herbal tea under darting dragonflies, and I recount my strange tale in full, sparing no detail. I talk about Brinklow and Pond, and the Banchini machine. The young woman is familiar (more or less) with these subjects. When I finish, she sits thinking for a time.

"I could give you some protective amulets and exorcism powder, but a situation like this calls for something stronger," Lauren says. "Are you familiar with Crocker's Bite?"

"I'm afraid not," I reply.

My hostess explains... A sprawling farm once stood on the outskirts of Kingston, Rhode Island. It was owned by a man named Gilbert Crocker. In the summer of 1860 a fierce storm pounded the area with thunder and rain. During the barrage, a bolt of lightning struck the heavy wooden door of the Crocker barn. Fortunately the structure did not burn, though a good-sized mark was left behind. The blackened area was roughly ovular in shape, and embedded within that charred wood were hundreds of human teeth.

Crocker, for whatever reason, felt that the teeth were a symbol of good luck, and over the years people dug them out of the door to carry for protection. In time, certain individuals found that the teeth possessed an even more dramatic power when used as a tool to dispel unwanted entities.

Lauren cites one case in particular, in which a family in Newport was terrorized by a hair-pulling boy-like thing in the winter of 1960. They eventually contacted a local medium, who utilized one of the teeth, successfully driving the bothersome spirit away.

My hostess goes into her house and returns with a small bag made of black cloth. Inside is what looks to be a yellowed human molar.

"A gift," the woman says.

I offer to pay her for it, but she assures me that she has others, and insists on its being a present. I accept her generosity and thank her profusely.

"So, what do I *do* with it?"

"Well, it's a close-quarters kind of thing," Lauren says, leaning forward in her lawn chair. "All you have to do is touch it to the target and that should do the trick."

"Touch it?" I ask, frowning. "I was hoping I wouldn't ever be close enough to that thing to touch it again."

Lauren has a way of being pleasant and dead serious all in the same breath. I respect her frankness, though her words cause me to shudder. "Well, situations arise against our will, and we're left to deal with them. You may not have a choice in the matter."

I hold the tooth in my hand, looking down at it. Lauren watches me, her face quiet and kind. I ask, "What should I do now?"

"Well, you could try to outrun it, I suppose, but if I were you, I'd just settle in someplace and let it come to you. Facing it will be less maddening than anticipating it."

This is all so surreal. A very bad dream in the middle of a beautiful September day. I sit here in the sunny garden and begin to laugh. Sometimes laughter is an expression of terror.

10. THE HOUSE OF 12 WHISPERS

Albert Pond hadn't felt quite right since his visit to the Banchini machine. His chest ached where he had received the blow from an unseen force, and he experienced vivid dreams of Victorian London, episodes that felt more like memories than dreams.

He had driven his Nash to a peculiar old house high in piney Maine. It was the place that Arcangelo Banchini had told him about -- The House of 12 Whispers.

The owner at that time was Abigail Winters, a reclusive old woman, relative of the man who had built the big brick Federal in Searsport, Maine.

Pond described the home: "The height and grandeur of the structure were emphasized by four tall chimneys which marked the corners of a hipped roof."

Captain Thomas Winters first occupied the building in the spring of 1798. He was as eccentric as he was wealthy, and given to obscure interests which included mummification. Winters possessed some degree of architectural ability and designed a unique room on the first floor of his dwelling.

"Miss Winters had consented to my visit, though I never did set eye upon her. She remained elsewhere in the house for the duration of my time there," Pond said.

The doctor was met by a grave and silvered male servant who escorted him to the strange chamber at the center of the first floor. The door was fitted with heavy locks, which the butler worked, one after the other, to allow the guest entry.

Pond addressed the older man. "I was told that I need not bother to ask any particular questions..."

"That's correct, sir. He'll tell you what you need to know," the butler said, swinging the door open.

The chamber is described in Pond's journal: "The room was circular and domed, an impressive example of brickwork that made me think of an oversized beehive oven. The floor, but for a raised brick path that led to the central feature, was entirely covered in all manner of seashells.

"A platform sat in the middle of the shells and on this stood an elongated upright dome of glass. A figure sat in a wing chair within the dome, facing me, its hands resting on its thighs. It was Captain Winters, dressed darkly and neatly, as a gentleman of his day would have dressed. He had been dead for many years, yet he was well preserved -- the result of some sort of mummification process.

"The skin on the face and hands was dark and leathery, with a slight sheen. It held tightly to the bones, making the corpus all the more ghastly. Wispy grey hair still clung to the head; combed back, it hung down to the top of his shirt collar."

Pond walked carefully along the brick path and stopped just short of the dome. Glass, and a matter of feet, stood between him and the cadaver. Its eyes were squinted shut and the mouth was wrapped around the small end of a copper funnel. The wide trumpet-mouth was pressed up against the glass.

The whole thing took only moments. Pond pressed his ear to the cool exterior of the dome, and a voice like rustling paper breathed from the funnel. Twelve words only. Each visitor received only twelve words.

"The sixth ocean lives -- go to The Garden of Guns -- save Earth"

11. GOOSEFLESH AND COAL SMOKE

Pond spent the night in Searsport, his rented room blurred by the haze of many cigarettes. His mind was too busy to tolerate sleep, so he paced and smoked late into the night.

He remembered how back in his home office the resinous baby had gotten onto Professor Wakefield's face and shaped an animated mask. The crude features had shown some resemblance to Simon Brinklow, and it had repeated "six oceans" over and over.

"Six oceans," Pond muttered to himself. There were only five oceans on the Earth. What was all this about six oceans, he wondered? He was particularly distressed by the way Captain Winters' message had ended with "save Earth."

"Save it from *what*?" The doctor asked no one.

Pond knew intuitively that the message referred to the planet, rather than earth, as in soil.

At least there was one piece of concise information sandwiched between the enigmatic bits... "The Garden of Guns" was clearly a place name; he determined to seek it out.

Meanwhile, the aching above Albert's solar plexus accentuated his inability to asleep. It was even beginning to distract him from his contemplation. At one point he went to a mirror, unbuttoned his shirt and had a look. Imagine his surprise when he saw a small fleshy protrusion crooking out from the center of his ribcage.

"It made me think of a plucked chicken wing," he wrote in his journal. And... "It twitched a little when I examined it."

The doctor had seen patients born with anomalies -- too few or too many fingers and other minor abnormalities, but he had never seen anything like this. Whatever it was, it did not appear to be wired into his nervous system, for it registered no feeling that he was aware of, even when he pinched it with his fingers.

Pond was terribly disturbed by his discovery, and more so over the next few days as the nubby thing continued to grow and shape. "By the third evening it had reached a length of thirteen inches, and the mass at the end bore five blunt knobs that caused me to think of nipples."

The new appendage was pale and contained bones. It grew longer and more distinct -- all the while, a city of damp coal smoke and horse-drawn carriages dominated Pond's dreams.

The man got very little done that week. He was exhausted and feverish, and not until the new arm had finished forming did his vigor and sharp-mindedness return. The curious dreams, and the pain, dissipated.

There was no mistaking what the thing was, for while it was thin and poorly colored, it was indeed a human arm and hand. A right hand. Pond thought that it looked frail, malnourished, stunted; either that or it was the limb of a child, for it reached only as far down as his navel.

"I have witnessed only a few demonstrations of animation," Pond recorded in his journal. "Every so often it shudders or twitches, and one chill evening I saw that the hairless forearm exhibited gooseflesh."

Pond tried poking the thing with a pin to see what sort of reaction he might get. He himself felt nothing, but the arm jerked appropriately and Pond spoke an apology aloud, though he felt rather foolish afterward. When his initial terror receded, he found himself both intrigued and befuddled. Had it been me, I'd have made a dash for the nearest hospital. I wish I possessed half the courage that Albert Pond had.

Obviously something *had* taken place back in Banchini's underground room, and the proof was that arm, hanging there limply, a bloodless lamprey fastened to his chest.

12. BULLETS AND BLOSSOMS

The Garden of Guns was tucked at the end of a winding dirt road on the tightrope between West Boylston and Worcester, in Massachusetts. Bordering vegetation encroached upon the path to the point where Pond eventually had to park his Nash and walk. The day was clear and bright, and before long he found himself standing in a wild garden of bees and blooms and misty summer heat.

Pond's observations: "I could not tell for certain if human hands had shaped the place, though it was distinct from the surrounding wood, a maze of wild rose bushes and early goldenrod, grape vines like winged nets cast over skeletons of birch."

A mossy path wound through clumps of shrubbery and patches of skulking thyme, browning spears of mullein and barbed thistle. There were daisies and coneflowers and Queen Anne's Lace with flowers like disks of foam.

Pond walked slowly amongst the scented brambles, his arms slack at his side, the third arm limp beneath his shirt. He would later write that he felt as if he were sleepwalking, and somehow knew just where to go. He stopped in front of a dense waist-high bush and waited.

The bush rustled as if a hidden bird had startled. Metallic light winked through the shadows and leaves -- something began to emerge from the foliage.

"I watched as a hand came up through the leaves like the head of a cobra. It was a pale hand, and its slender fingers were wrapped around a silvery antique pistol, offering it to me butt-first. I reached down and accepted the smooth ivory handle as the fingers released. The hand slid back into the shade, whispering through the foliage.

"I examined the weapon; it was gracefully primitive, a nickel-plated pocket revolver from the late eighteen-seventies. The cylinder was loaded -- the bullets poking out from their shell casings were cast from a strange coppery metal, and imprinted with a vague texture that made me think of fish scales. I held the pistol up in the sunlight. It gleamed like Excalibur."

13. THE PUZZLING JOURNAL

It was at about that time, nearing the end of summer in 1920, that Pond's journal became convoluted. The entries from then are often spotty, descriptively speaking, and less frequent overall. When the handwritten original made its way into the hands of his friend, Nigel Wagner (who later published it), entire pages were missing.

This final section of the journal has always compelled me the most, even though I find it unnerving. The fact that there are missing parts to the story just adds to the appeal for me. His travels are like the Loch Ness Monster in that they dip down into dark waters, so to speak, tantalizing, making us eager to learn more, or to get a better look. I suppose it's like burlesque in that sense. How interested would we really be in Nessie if she were stuffed, stretched out in a glass case at a Scottish museum, her mystery expunged by genetic science?

The journal does inform us that Pond did quite a bit of traveling in late August and early September, putting many miles on his trustworthy Nash. The old-fashioned pistol accompanied him, tucked in his waistband. He only shares glimpses of some places; for instance, the site called Burnt Stream. The preceding page was gone, so I have no way of knowing what New England state Burnt Stream was (or is) in. In the published version of the journal Wagner inserted blank pages to signify where leaves in the original were absent.

At any rate, Pond wrote: " -- detected a certain charred smell by the banks of the fast, ash-colored water. On the night in question, the farmer heard strange noises coming from the wood that encloses the stream. He imitated the high, hollow sound, and I was put in mind of coyotes, which, he insisted, were not responsible for the cries.

"Back at his house, I examined the dark lengths of seemingly human hair, and the photographs of other things he had fished from the water...the small copper fish, and the larger oddity, like the emaciated grey torso of a two-year-old child, all ribs and slick tendrils. It looked as if it never had possessed a head. The creature had survived for several days, the old man told me; it lay there on his sofa with its multiple limbs whipping, slowing in their movements as it darkened and died and eventually turned into what he called tar."

Pond's host took a photograph of him, the last known picture ever taken of the doctor. It is the picture I now possess, along with the burnt image of Arabella's baby. I purchased them for a hefty price at the annual auction held by the little-known Society of Esoteric Antiquities.

The photograph shows a man who had seen much, a man who had suffered war and loss. Yet his eyes revealed an unflinching determination. Turning back was not a consideration.

Pond was in New Hampshire on the sixth of September. He stayed at a Concord hotel which, he suspected, contained a speakeasy in its cellar. His amazing new protuberance, secreted beneath his garments, had remained inactive throughout his recent travels, spare the occasional tremor.

He had contemplated the arm thoroughly. It was fairly obvious that he had picked up an internal passenger, or part of one, from Banchini's machinery. It had proven harmless so far. He was thankful for that, for there was little chance of getting away from it but for amputation, the possibility of which he had discarded early on. He wondered if the dreams of London were an indication of the arm's identity.

Of his night in Concord, his journal entry goes as follows... "At some point in my sleep I was vaguely aware of fingers delicately exploring my face, as if a blind person were trying to recognize me."

The journal goes on to show that Pond had encounters with wondrous beauty, as well as things unsettling. Pausing at the home of Brady Cushing Lodge, amidst the coloring hills of Glastenbury, Vermont, he had the opportunity to listen to the Ring of Masks.

Brady was a man of many interests, ranging from astronomy and archaeology to anthropology and necromancy. He had spent a great deal of time digging along the Green Mountain range -- an area popular with treasure hunters, despite the fact that Vermont is not by the sea and thus would be an unlikely source of pirate's gold. Burrowing under the shadows and stones of South Mountain, Lodge made a fascinating discovery. He unearthed a circular stone-lined pit containing seven clay masks of undeterminable age.

The masks were not quite like anything he had seen before, and, considering his anthropological expertise, he was familiar with the stylistic particulars of masks found worldwide. These artifacts certainly did not appear to be the work of indigenous peoples.

The masks all looked alike, although some were better preserved than others. They were pale, smooth but for chips and cracks, with no mouths indicated. The noses were understated, and the eyes were dark mussel shells, apparently pressed into the clay faces while they were still soft.

Rather than simply hoard his find, Lodge sought guidance through necromantic communications (automatic writing) and constructed a curious device which integrated the clay faces... The Ring of Masks resembled a chandelier in a way; it was a skeletal thing of dark metal arms, suspended from a rotating mechanism which nestled under the ceiling of a small dark room no bigger than a pantry. The masks were attached to the thin arms, facing inward, facing each other.

Dr. Pond sat in a chair as this bizarre contraption was lowered down to encircle his head. He found himself eye to eye with one of the inscrutably gazing masks, then with another as they gradually began to rotate. Less than a foot from his face, they continued to spin faster, the speed increasing as the device dictated until they were whirling dizzily, the pale faces blurring, the dark shell eyes smudging upon the air like an unbroken bar of black.

"Mesmerizing as the imagery was," Pond wrote, "it was the *sound* that I heard which made the greatest impression on me. Hushed at first, it increased in volume as the faces moved faster around my head. Their whispers merged into something that I have never heard before, and I am haunted by the memory...

"It was a million drowning heartbeats swept along in a single note -- a river, a wind -- the song of dark seas dreaming. A dirge of moonlight reborn in a sunken temple.

"I feel that I would be insulting this music if I were to try and confine it further with human language, so I will only say this: it was the most beautiful sound ever to enter my ears.

"While there was no actual information for me to take away and decipher from this experience, on some level I suddenly knew that I was approaching the end of my quest."

The journal pages marking the first week of October are missing -- a blank sheet represents them. A series of brief entries follow...

"Oct. 9th, 1920: Tunnels under old brick church in Hancock, New Hampshire."

Pond lists no particular state for the site he visited on Oct. 12th. I have not been able to locate the spot on contemporary or archaic maps. The entry reads: "Oct. 12th, 1920: Oddmeadow, where the moon is seen to move in reverse."

By mid-month he was in Massachusetts... "Oct. 16th, 1920: Old Burying Ground, Barnstable. Knox grave. Read epitaph backward by moonlight. It spelled END OF THE WORLD."

It's likely that Pond is referring to the grave of Capt. Duncan Knox, whose schooner, the Catherine Hope, went down off Block Island in the spring of 1856. Incredibly, the Captain's body washed up on the distant Cape Cod Bay not two hours later, his mouth filled with clumps of long white hair.

Pond was obviously employing some kind of mysterious technique at the cemetery, for the epitaph when read in reverse is actually a nonsensical jumble.

In the journal the publisher noted that part of one page from the late October section was torn away, thus the following entry appears incomplete: "--decrepit, abandoned for many years. House sits amidst overgrown fields of dull autumn grass and weeds. Upstairs, northern bedchamber -- looking out window saw a vast expanse of stormy grey water. Lowering sky above a horizon of milky luminescence. Water came up to the edge of second-floor panes. Small boat tossed on waves, passed window just feet away. Lone occupant was naked old man, crouched or half-standing. Grey skin, emaciated. Dark screeching birds fastened to him head to foot by rusty spikes.

"When I opened the sash of the window the view appeared ordinary -- nothing but the overgrown fields."

It's been speculated that Pond was writing of the Parson Ezekiel Littlefield House in Middleborough, Massachusetts (no longer standing) where the cleric was rumored to keep a mysterious young woman captive in an upstairs chamber. Then, toward the end of the month, the name Arabella reappears. Pond had visited an art show featuring the work of a promising Boston portrait artist who had recently gone missing. One image in particular caught Pond's attention... Norris Sarde had painted a naked woman with dark hair lying on a damp grey beach at the base of a looming stone temple. It was entitled The Sixth Ocean.

None of Sarde's acquaintances could offer Pond much information regarding the woman who had posed for the artist. Only one of them had met her, and that individual could not recall the woman uttering a single word. "She never smiled either," the witness reflected. He was sure that Sarde had mentioned his model's name at the time, but he could not remember what it was.

We can only wonder about some of the adventures Pond experienced and what he might have learned from them. He certainly had his reasons for going to Oddmeadow, the graveyard, the parson's house and the tunnels under an old New Hampshire church (and who knows where else). We are also left to speculate as to how he came across the exhibition of Norris Sarde's work. Somewhere along the way he uncovered an odd way of locating individuals. He made use of the procedure at Nantasket Beach on October 20th.

In preparation for the ritual, Pond procured two handfuls of black sunflower seeds. These were placed inside a hollowed-out turnip. He replaced the lid of the organic vessel, sealed it with wax, then placed it in a pot of milk. He slept with the pot under his bed.

At the next high tide -- which happened to be the following morning -- he went down to the sea and knelt at the edge of the nudging waves. He opened the gourd and sprinkled the seeds into the surf. They floated, dispersed and were carried out to sea.

Pond passed the time in a hotel room. Shortly before low tide he returned to the spot where he had deposited the seeds. Dusk was falling, and there was moisture in the sea air -- lighter than drizzle, more dappling than mist. He knelt by the shore, watching the ashen foam as the waves slid back. The reversing water revealed damp sand, and pressed into the surface of the sand were the sunflower seeds. They were arranged in such a way as to spell out asymmetric words... They gave a location, a date and a time.

14. RETURN TO LEXINGTON

Anticipating the return of the white-haired figure has left my nerves in a fragile state. I shy at sudden sounds, and my entire body clenches each time a person with long light hair enters my periphery. My appetite is compromised, and my hands have adopted a chronic tremble. I am, by nature, anything but a combative creature...I dread the inevitable confrontation.

The small black bag containing the tooth remains in my pocket at all times. It offers some slight degree of comfort, but wouldn't I feel stronger if I were armed with a pistol as Pond was? I suppose I could venture to the site where The Garden of Guns once grew, but that in itself might prove dangerous. A low-income housing project was built on the spot back in the mid-seventies. Since then the complex of dreary brick boxes has become infested with drugs and criminals. In fact, there are a disproportionate number of shootings there in the tenements, and interestingly enough, many of the weapons involved are antiques.

I suppose it is possible that the thing that followed me from New Hampshire has lost interest in me. If it were truly intent on locating me wouldn't it have done so by now? Couldn't it have done me harm right there outside the Eastborough library if it had been so inclined?

I mustn't talk myself into a false sense of security. There have been some terrible deaths related to the phenomenon of overlaps, as well as the disappearances. Poor Professor Wakefield certainly suffered a disturbing end there in Pond's examination office, and then there was the Rosemary Willard case of 1969.

Roy and Rosemary Willard were a married couple living in a working-class neighborhood of Bridgeport, Connecticut. It was the end of July, and they had just returned from a vacation trip to Cape Cod. Roy had done some fishing on the Cape -- he caught a small coppery fish the likes of which he had never seen. It broke like glass when it squirmed from his hands and landed on the deck of the boat.

After the couple unpacked, so the story goes, Roy went upstairs to take a bath. His wife remained downstairs; she heard the water running for an unnaturally long time and wondered if her husband had fallen asleep with the faucet on. She went upstairs and knocked at the bathroom door but received no answer. She knocked louder and called to her husband, but still he did not reply. Finally she opened the door and looked in.

The floor was flooded. Roy was slumped on his back in the overflowing tub with a small grey person the size of a cat crouching on his chest. The creature had its arms wrapped around the oversized handle of a black metal tool reminiscent of a garden spade. It was scooping out a large hole where her husband's face had been, hollowing out his head as if it were a jack-o'-lantern.

Rosemary ran from the house and was found screaming in the street. When the police came, she told them what she saw. It was obvious to them that she had gone mad and killed the man. She was arrested for murder and placed in jail to await trial.

Several weeks later Rosemary vanished from her cell. The compartment did not appear compromised in any way, and yet she was gone. All that the authorities found were a few briny strands of black seaweed strewn on the floor.

Is it any wonder that I can't eat or sleep?

I have returned to Lexington, to the noble old Sumner Inn. Somehow, looming against a backdrop of colorful maples, it seems older than when I last saw it. But autumn has a way of making all of New England seem a glorious and haunted antique.

It is good to be in the warming company of Imogene Carlisle. She feeds me, seats me by the fire and pours me tea. I am comfortable enough to tell her about my travels and my encounter with the ghastly stranger.

She is a steady woman as well as self-sufficient. She reassures me that I will be fine. But, I wonder if those are merely the obligatory words of a good-hearted individual -- didn't I see a look of fear flicker in her eyes?

It is late, and I am sitting in my room. This is the same one in which I stayed last time. A soft September rain pads at the window, and wind breathes through the wet leaves. I am steeling myself. A flashlight, an umbrella and an empty glass bottle are waiting on the bed.

Not knowing where to turn, I have decided to summon Fractured Harry. He, or it, will guide me, suggest a location where I should go -- maybe someplace to escape the thing that stole into this realm, or maybe someplace to find it. I have memorized the strange little conjuration song; I whisper it into the bottle. I cork the bottle and slip it into my raincoat. I leave my room, walk quietly through the old Georgian inn and step out into the rain.

The old cemetery is a short walk down the road. Raindrops wink in the beam of my flashlight; others dapple my umbrella. The burial yard is shapeless in the dark. The old tilted slates regard me inscrutably with their carved faces. Wet leaves squeak and hiss under my feet, wet leaves scent the air. I bend, stuff the bottle into damp grass and head back to the inn.

15. THE RECITAL

The seeds in the sand showed Pond where to go. It was the evening of October 30th, 1920. He drove west through rain and falling leaves, through a tunnel of soggy trees. He reached the humble center of Sterling, Massachusetts, found the old meetinghouse and parked the Nash.

Other vehicles were crowded outside the big white building; lights filled the tall windows. Pond could hear music coming from inside, moody strings humming, rumbling like the thunder that the storm did not provide.

Pond was wearing his finest suit. He adjusted his shirt to better hide the extra limb, straightened his tie, then climbed the granite steps. The large double doors whined as he entered the lobby. A sign on an easel announced a free chamber music recital by the local composer Davis Storrow.

Rich tones filled the old 1850s structure, warming it. There were cello chords so deep that they nearly vibrated through the floor. Pond followed the sounds, his fast heart contrasting with the pensive flow of music. He came to an open doorway and peered in. The audience was a modest crowd, largely obscured in dimness; a string quartet was seated on a small stage.

Pond scanned the audience for Arabella. Many women were wearing hats, but she was not -- he knew her by her black hair; even from behind, he knew. She was in the front row. The music piece came to an end and the hall was briefly silent. Someone suppressed a cough. Old floorboards creaked under Pond's nervous shifting.

The lead violinist stood up and smiled. He was handsome and rather young with a thin mustache, his hair slicked back and dark. It was Davis Storrow.

"Now," Storrow said, gazing into the front row, a certain intimate quality in his manner informing Pond that the performer was holding the eye of a lover, "we will be performing my latest composition, entitled *Daughter of the Drowned Temple.*"

Pond stepped forward as the first bow touched its strings. High notes. Storrow played well -- the sound conjured a mental image of moonlight shimmering on water. Pond was through the doorway and in the hall proper. The cello came in; it moaned with a rhythm like slow waves. Pond walked along one side of the audience, staring at the back of Arabella's head.

It was a lovely piece of music, steady and building as Pachelbel's *Canon.* Storrow was rapt. The music was suffused with beauty and sadness as it filled the air. Pond moved through it as if wading in water. He was nearing the front row.

He did not know what he would say to her, or if she would even remember him. Was she now capable of speech? *What* in fact was she? He had succeeded in finding her, and yet, as he closed the distance between them, he found himself wondering, "what next?"

The strings dipped, hauntingly low. Arabella's profile came into view. The doctor's shadow swept over her, and she turned, looked up as he stepped in front of her. She was as beautiful as he remembered, her eyes darker than black, a striking contrast to her flesh, her pearls and her simple white dress.

"Hello," he said.

Arabella grinned pleasantly and tilted her head. He saw the recognition register, and something else entirely as the small third arm darted out from his shirt, snatched the pistol from his waistband and fired into her face.

Pond was as surprised as the rest.

"No!" he cried.

Arabella jolted back in her seat, then slumped forward, her head hanging down so that black hair made a veil around the damage. A stream of liquid poured down, darkening her dress. It was greyish, translucent, and it smelled like the sea.

There was a terrible commotion, women screaming, people tumbling and running. Pond bent to try and aid Arabella. The fragile little hand had dropped the silver gun; it reached to touch the woman's face. It stroked her wet cheek with a tenderness that seemed apologetic.

Several men rushed at Pond and pinned him to the ground. Davis Storrow came raging, wielding his violin like a club. Arabella was the only one left sitting in the audience, slack amongst the tipped chairs. The bleeding had stopped suddenly, as if a faucet that had been shut off.

16. A MEETING OF SORTS

Pond was charged with murder and placed in the only cell that the little Sterling police station possessed. Numb, and bruised from his capture, he sat on the bunk staring at the floor. He had not even bothered to try to explain that the small freak arm had acted of its own accord.

They had left Pond his journal and his pen, but he felt hollow inside and incapable of words. Although he was not a violent man, he found himself wishing that he had removed the third arm. He found himself wanting to kill it.

Pond felt something tap his shoulder. He looked down -- it was the little pale arm. It pointed to the journal that sat beside him on the bunk. It also pointed to the pen.

"You want to write?"

The doctor was both incredulous and intrigued. He was hesitant about giving the thing a sharp object, but he handed it the pen nonetheless. He remained ready to subdue it if it made any threatening moves.

Pond opened the journal to a blank page. He had to hold it up so that the short protrusion could reach it with the pen. The doctor read as the little hand wrote.

"My dear Dr. Pond, there are not words enough to express my regrets in regards to this dreadful situation. Please allow me to explain. The creature you called Arabella was, in actual fact, a walking ocean. The Sixth Ocean. Poor thing had no choice in the matter, mind you, but upon her death, be it natural, accidental or by some pistol other than that exceptional one which you had procured, her form, as it was, would have unleashed an unborn ocean to flood the world as we know it. Imagine if she had taken a fatal tumble down a staircase, or been trampled by one of those queer horse-less carriages? Arabella would have been the end of the world."

The journal trembled in Pond's hands.

"But, all that has been corrected, though the method and the results were indeed unfortunate. I should like to have had the opportunity to explain this all in advance. However, interred as I am in your body, I have only recently achieved a satisfactory quality of cognizance, and mastering my dreadful little appendage has proven no small feat. It is perhaps fortuitous that I was capable of taking action when the opportunity arrived. Please forgive the lack of due warning.

"I should like to add that I have observed you to be a gentleman of honor, and an adventurer of the highest caliber. I tip my hat to you, Dr. Pond."

Then the hand signed its name.

"Yours sincerely, Simon Brinklow."

Pond stared at the words, dazed. He recognized the signature.

"Heavens," he muttered, "it *is* you."

The hand gave Pond the pen, then hung in the air, offering its palm.

Pond gently shook the little hand. "Mr. Brinklow, it's an honor to meet you."

17. VISITATION

I close *Dr. Pond's Journal* and put it down on the bed.

They found his cell empty in the morning. He had disappeared, though the confining chamber was intact. There was nothing to be found but his journal and pen and a few limp strands of slippery black sea rack. Neither the authorities, nor anyone else for that matter, ever found Dr. Albert Pond.

It has been more than an hour since I left the bottle at the little graveyard. I have once again finished reading Pond's book. I've lost count of how many times I've read it. This time it thrills and terrifies me even more than the first time I read it. I am about to experience something that he, and Brinklow before him, experienced, an earnest contact with another realm...a visit from Fractured Harry.

The rain has persisted; in fact it has increased if anything. Several times I have mistaken its sounds for the noise of a figure moving about in the darkness outside the house. Once I even thought that I heard the distant door in the main entryway open and close. I actually shuddered at the sound, and I find my hands trembling still, even though there is no evidence whatsoever that Harry is anything but a benevolent spirit.

It is nearly two in the morning, and I am sitting here like a frightened boy in this ancient house. How small I feel, stripped of the security of disbelief. It is an aching thing to know that we are all so tiny, stumbling in a universe that is wider and darker than any Earth-bound sea.

Two-fifteen and I hear the first footstep. Rain patters in the leaves outside. The second step, like the first, is soft, a measured pressure on the old floor planks. Others follow -- they are too quiet to echo in the hall outside my room.

A single knock at the door. I have left the door unlocked. I startle, jolt up from the bed. Another knock, just a bit louder this time.

"Come in," I call softly.

A third knock. A fourth. I step toward the door. I remember that Brinklow and Pond both opened the door for Harry -- I must do the same. I reach for the door -- it slides open several inches before I can touch the knob.

A pale hand grasps my wrist! The grip is icy, and the fingernails are tiny white trilobites. I cry out and jerk free, stumbling back toward the bed as the door swings wide.

The creature has white hair -- wet leaves tangled in the hair. It is naked, thin as an upright greyhound, smiling a toothless smile.

I fumble a hand into my pocket, grope for the small black bag.

It speaks -- a voice that is several wound together like the threads of a string. A wintry, thin sound...

"Have you no manners? You can't even say hello to an old friend? This is the second time you've stung me with your impudence..."

The figure steps fully into the room and pushes the door shut behind it. Hair obscures the eyes.

"Haven't you realized that I was only going to thank you back at the library? I was going to thank you for letting me out. But you scorned me." The black mouth twists around its words, "A pity. You can't expect me to let a slight like that go unpunished."

The creature raises one wrinkled hand to the height of my face and advances as I pull the bag from my pocket and throw it. A direct hit in the chest. Voices shrill. It dances backward and folds to the floor. I hear an electric crackling sound as the pale mass jerks then goes still, its limbs folded in as if it is a dead spider.

"Pain," voices hiss. "Terrible pain!"

The being shoots up from the floor. It is partly fragmented; there are gaps in the torso that I can see through, and others filled with dull flashes of light, and what look to be weaving swarms of tiny flies. One arm seems to be connected by nothing more than twitching pixels.

"You hurt me," the thing's voices rasp. "I'm afraid I'm going to have to kiss you now..." It reaches up and flicks the long white hair away from its face, revealing the eye sockets. There are no eyes, only gouges from which twin masses of small jointed legs, like those of a crab or a trilobite, protrude. The legs quaver and flex as the ghastly figure prepares to pounce.

The door behind the monster swings open and a jerky figure with a pumpkin for a head lunges from behind. Its body is a plaid bathrobe, the bloated fingers are bunches of colorful Indian corn. It wraps its arms around the naked creature and the two figures grapple.

Fractured Harry hooks his fingers into the holes in the other, and bursts of light widen the wounds. The grey thing shudders and shrieks as an arm falls off and breaks like white ash on the floor. Chunks of chest follow, then the legs and hips. The upper body rips and tumbles, then the screeching head -- white hair trailing like the tail of a comet -- it falls to the floor and breaks.

The cries fly away like birds and fade until the only sound is the rain tapping its meaningless code on the window. I sink to the edge of the bed, gasping and feverish. Fractured Harry stands above the powdery stains, facing me. He bows stiffly. His corncob fingers are scorched black and smoking. I look up at his pumpkin head.

"Thank you," I manage.

Harry takes a step closer and leans down. His words are an alien whisper, a meaning that I receive just the same. He tells me the name of the place where I must go. Home.

18. DUSK

The first snow of the season is falling. It wanders down the grey November sky and settles on yards and roofs, finds grooves in the limbs of naked maple trees. It brushes the windowpane, each flake unique, each a ghostly fingerprint.

I am listening to a rare recording of Davis Storrow's *Daughter of the Drowned Temple*. It is the first time that I have actually heard the piece, and I find it as lovely and haunting as Pond had described it to be. It actually gives me chills.

These last few weeks have been pleasantly uneventful. I've kept to myself, safe in my small house in Grafton, snug in a womb of tea steam and Nana's old books.

What of Pond and Brinklow? There are those who claim that they have uncovered traces of them, like the eccentric fellow in Vermont who insists that he found their initials carved on a rotten old board that washed up on the shore of Lake Champlain. Down in Sturbridge, Massachusetts there's a structure that Pond aficionados refer to as The Trilobite House because the frost that appears on the windows looks distinctly like those strange prehistoric creatures. Witnesses have even claimed to see three handprints shaped by ice on the panes -- two of normal size, with one small one in between. Then there's the Mt. Desert Photo, a grainy, half-focused snapshot taken atop a mountain in Maine that purportedly shows a portly fellow in Victorian garb and a dashing fellow in 1920s attire standing on a ledge, gazing out over a misty expanse of sea and distant islands.

The music ends. I am pensive, too comfortable to get up and put anything else on. The snow has stopped, having left little more than a dusting. I continue to look out the window. The sky clears, but for some of those brooding purple-grey clouds so characteristic of November in these parts.

The days go dark so early now. The tree shadows reach to each other and merge, and the moon comes up, as if released from some forgotten stone temple, as if born of an ash-colored sea.

End

Afterword

Jeffrey Thomas

My brother Scott Thomas' story *The Sea of Ash* has a rather convoluted back-story.

A decade ago now, publisher Sean Wallace of Prime Books had a brainstorm. He was very enamored of a piece of artwork by Travis Anthony Soumis (who has done covers for a number of my books), called *Dreams Are Dark*, which portrays a woman lying supine in the surf, with her arms spread wide like wings, while in the distance a strange pillared building looms against a moody sky. Sean asked if Scott and I could each write a novella inspired by the same image, to be collected in one book with Travis' art serving as the cover. We agreed to this unique challenge, and Scott came up with the book's title: *The Sea of Flesh and Ash*. One of us would write a story called *The Sea of Flesh*, the other *The Sea of Ash*. I confessed I wanted the flesh, Scott admitted he had hoped for the ash, and so with title and Travis' image in hand, we went our separate ways to write our stories in solitude, without sharing anything with the other about our respective stories until they were finished.

After this promising beginning, however, the project stalled, and remained in limbo for a number of years. While we were both grateful to Sean for inspiring our stories, which wouldn't have come into existence without him, and fully understanding the difficulties and vagaries of indie press publishing, ultimately we felt we needed to find a new home for the book so that it could finally reach the hands of readers who had been hearing about it, and anticipating it, for years.

So in 2011, we decided to take a chance on a new publisher called Terradan Works, and the book was finally released with its intended cover art (though Travis updated it slightly).

Though Terradan published a lovely looking book, it's often hard for a beginner publisher to reach out and garner sufficient notice for their titles, and so in an effort to gain a wider audience for my novella *The Sea of Flesh*, in 2013 I included it in my short story collection *Worship the Night*, separate from Scott's novella. I encouraged Scott to see that *The Sea of Ash* was likewise reprinted somewhere, to reach the readership it deserved. Thus, I was overjoyed when Mike Davis, of the widely esteemed *Lovecraft eZine*, read Scott's story, fell in love with it, and decided to reprint it in digital and print formats -- gushing that it was one of the finest stories he had ever read.

Indeed, the wildly inventive and intricately constructed *The Sea of Ash* may very well be Scott's masterpiece to date, and that says a lot when you're talking about a writer who was selected by Karl Edward Wagner to be included in the final edition of DAW's *The Year's Best Horror Stories*, and who once saw *two* of his stories selected by Ellen Datlow for a single volume of *The Year's Best Fantasy and Horror*. Scott's stories typically take place in an 18th or 19th Century New England or UK (or in some alternate reality version of either), and as such they are impeccably researched. Scott's work is very much informed by his love of classic horror literature, most notably the great M. R. James, and yet it is highly original. Typical of Scott's fiction is an astounding level of fantastical imagination bordering on the surreal, abounding with imagery and concepts as poetically beautiful as they are eerily disturbing. Another prominent feature of much of Scott's work is his love of nature, and how the natural world factors into his stories -- this, and the tragic plotlines of many of his tales, calling to mind Thomas Hardy.

Having read *The Sea of Ash*, I believe you will feel that its release to a wide audience was worth the long wait, and you will understand why Mike Davis stepped in to champion it. I envy you your first encounter with this novella. Indeed, if this is your first encounter with any of the fiction of my younger brother, I envy you all the more.

Biography

Scott Thomas' short story collections include *Urn and Willow, Midnight in New England, Quill and Candle, Westermead, The Garden of Ghosts, Cobwebs and Whispers* and *Over The Darkening Fields*. His novel *Fellengrey* is a fantastical nautical adventure set in an alternate 18th century Britain. Thomas lives in New England.

Made in the USA
Charleston, SC
07 January 2015